Praise for
The Legend of Bagger Vance

"*The Legend of Bagger Vance* is such
an entertaining book on the surface you hardly realize
you are being taught some of life's greatest truths.
Pressfield has seamlessly brought together that rare
combination of fun and enlightenment in a novel that
seems destined to take its place alongside some of
the great works in golf literature."
—*Links* magazine

"Entertaining, well crafted. . . . One need only have a
nodding acquaintance with the game of golf to enjoy
and appreciate this book; for the golfer . . . this is a
wonderful story—simply, a must-read."
—*Golfing* magazine

"Truly a delight. Even now when I play in
professional tournaments I think of the positive
effect Bagger Vance had on everyone associated with
him. He will be with me for many years to come."
—Patty Sheehan, member of the LPGA Hall of Fame

"Pure magic! I read it straight through in one sitting.
It should be required reading for anyone who
loves the game and has a sense of its history
and its mystery."
—Deane Beman, former commissioner of the PGA Tour

"The *Field of Dreams* of golf. . . . The only golf
novel ever written that earns 'couldn't put it down'
accolades. This is a book that will remain with
readers for a while, and will certainly emerge every
time they step on a golf course."
—*BookPage*

THE
LEGEND OF
BAGGER VANCE

a novel of golf and
the game of
life

STEVEN PRESSFIELD

WILLIAM MORROW
An Imprint of HarperCollinsPublishers

Special thanks to Larry, Jody, Sterling, Rich,
Lawrence of the Links and
to our own Essex girl, Christy (she knows why),
the Cowboy for flying to the rescue,
and, for steering me through Sanskrit,
Dr. Bruce Cameron Hall.

First Avon edition published 1996.

Reprinted in Perennial 2003.

Library of Congress Cataloging-in-Publication Data is available.

ISBN 0-380-72751-X

ScoutAutomatedPrintCode

Lt. William James Torpie, U.S. Army
October 20, 1943–March 25, 1969

For you, Billy,
and other friends who fell
on other fields

Tell me, Sanjaya, of the warriors' deeds
On that day when my sons faced the sons of Pandu,
Eager to do battle on the field of Kuru,
On the field of valor.

—*Bhagavad-Gita*

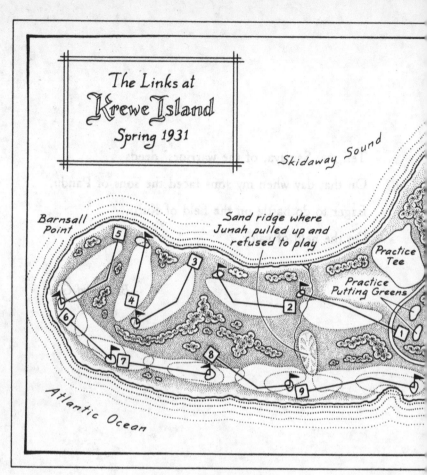

The Links at
Krewe Island
Spring 1931

Skidaway Sound

Barnsall
Point

Sand ridge where
Junah pulled up and
refused to play

Practice
Tee

Practice
Putting Greens

Atlantic Ocean

HOLE	NAME	CHAMPIONSHIP TEES		PAR	HANDICAP
1	Vigilance	521	yards	5	11
2	Sagacity	390	yards	4	13
3	Fortitude	325	yards	4	7
4	Prowess	194	yards	3	17
5	Rigor	378	yards	4	15
6	Temerity	230	yards	3	3
7	Cunning	405	yards	4	9
8	Might	442	yards	4	5
9	Faith	590	yards	5	1
OUT		3475	yards	36	

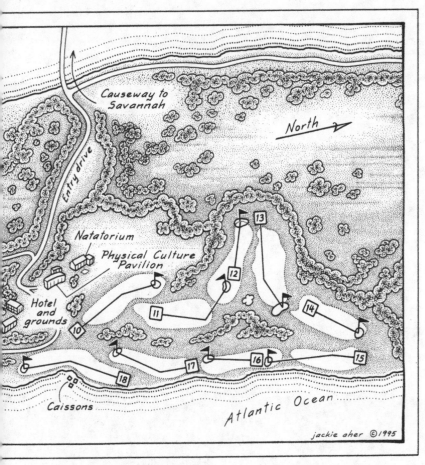

Causeway to Savannah

North

Natatorium

Physical Culture Pavilion

Hotel and grounds

Caissons

Atlantic Ocean

Entry drive

jackie aher ©1995

HOLE	NAME	CHAMPIONSHIP TEES		PAR	HANDICAP
10	Vigor	464	yards	4	6
11	Acumen	315	yards	4	14
12	Ingenuity	167	yards	3	8
13	Love	445	yards	4	18
14	Discipline	183	yards	3	10
15	Stamina	510	yards	5	16
16	Audacity	310	yards	4	12
17	Prudence	444	yards	4	4
18	Valor	541	yards	5	2
IN		3379	yards	36	
TOTAL		6854	yards	72	

THE
LEGEND OF
BAGGER VANCE

A Note to the Reader

I N MAY OF 1931 an exhibition match was held over 36 holes between the two greatest golfers of their day, Walter Hagen and Robert Tyre "Bobby" Jones, Jr. The match was the second and last between the two immortals (Hagen shelled Jones, 12 and 11 over 72 holes, at the first in Sarasota, Florida, in 1926). This second match was held at what was, at the time, the most costly and ambitious golf layout ever built in America, the Links at Krewe Island, Georgia.

Much has been written about the rather odd events of that long day. We have Grantland Rice's dispatches to the *New York Tribune,* which were published at that time. The notes and diaries of O. B. Keeler devote several quite absorbing pages to the match. And of course the reports from the dozens of newspapers and sporting journals that covered the event.

One aspect of that day, however, has been largely overlooked, or rather treated as a footnote, an oddity or sideshow. I refer to the inclusion in the competition, at the insistence of the citizens of Savannah, of a local champion, who in fact held his own quite honorably with the two golfing titans.

I was fortunate enough to witness that match, aged ten, from the privileged and intimate vantage of assisting the local champion's caddie. I was present for many of the events leading up to the day, for the match itself, as well as certain previously unrecorded adventures in its aftermath.

For many years, it has been my intention to commit my memory of these events to paper. However, a long and crowded career as a physician, husband and father of six has prevented me from finding the time I felt the effort deserved.

In candor, another factor has made me reluctant to make public these recollections. That is the rather fantastical aspect of a number of the events of that day. I was afraid that a true accounting would be misinterpreted or, worse, disbelieved. The facts, I feared, would either be discounted as the product of a ten-year-old's overactive imagination or, when perceived as the recollections of a man past seventy, be dismissed as burnished and embellished reminiscences whose truth has been lost over time in the telling and retelling.

The fact is, I have never told this story. Portions I have recounted to my wife in private; fragments have been imparted on specific occasion to my children. But I have never retold the story, to others or even to myself, in its entirety.

Until recently, that is. Attempting to counsel a troubled young friend, for whom I felt the tale might have significance, I passed an entire night, till sunrise, recounting the story verbally.

A Note to the Reader

It made such a profound impression on my young friend that I decided at last to try my hand at putting it down in written form.

This volume is that attempt.

I have chosen, for reasons which will become apparent, to tell the tale much as I recounted it that night. It is a story of a type of golfer, and a type of golf, which I fear have long since vanished from the scene. But I intend this record not merely as an exercise in reminiscence or nostalgia. For the events of that day had profound and far-reaching consequences on me and on others who participated, particularly the local champion referred to above.

His name was Rannulph Junah, and Bagger Vance was his caddie.

—HARDISON L. GREAVES, M.D.
Savannah, Georgia
March 1995

One

HAVE YOU EVER had blackjack tea, Michael? The real stuff, I mean. One of my patients gave me these, cured sassafras root from Plaquemines Parish in Louisiana. Something mysterious and potent about it. Clears the head. You can stay up all night with your brain so lucid it almost feels transparent. Smell the earth in it? Something about tea from roots, as opposed to leaves. Something deeper, more connected to the source. I remember that rooty, woodsy smell from winter mornings as a boy. My mother said only a Yankee or a fool sweetened blackjack tea with sugar. It had to be molasses. And no milk. The farthest afield she'd stray was to serve it *au citron*, like the Creoles. But I'm wandering already, and you've barely even sat down.

How are you, young man? No doubt you're expecting a lecture, but I promise that's the last thing I intend. Your decision to leave medical school is your own entirely. I can even understand and sympathize. Around the third year, when exhaustion and nausea have taken up permanent residence in your bones, the healing profession seems less like a calling and more like an exercise in expedience and venality. I understand that brand of despair better than I wish. But it's a different decision you've made that troubles me more deeply.

I mean your choice to give up golf.

When I heard, Michael, I knew something was wrong. Seriously wrong. That's why I've asked you here tonight.

Will you stay and listen to an old man?

You see, I know you better than you think. Not just from those forlorn "interviews" you endured once a year with the Scholarship Committee. In fact I made up my mind about you years earlier.

Do you remember when you used to caddie for me, in your "rabbit" days, when you were ten or eleven? You used to swing clubs on the tee like the other boys, but there was something that struck me particularly about you. You had an instinct. You saw through to the soul of the game.

Frank the caddiemaster told me once how, at ten years old, you asked to be sent out only with the best players, just so you could watch and learn. Frank showed me the list you gave him. Do you remember? The list of your approved players. I was flattered to find my own name on it.

I used to watch you sometimes when you weren't looking. What struck me particularly was your interest in the grip. You knew, like every real expert, that a true player can be recognized by his grip alone. The way a man sets his hands on a club will inform you infallibly as to how deeply he's thought about the game, how profoundly he's entered into its mysteries.

The grip, a remarkable fellow named Bagger Vance once told me, when I was about the same age you were then, is man's connection to the world outside himself. The hands, he said, are where the subjective meets the objective. Where we "in here" meet the world "out there." True intelligence, Vance declared, does not reside in the brain, but in the hands.

You had a wonderful grip. Even as a little boy, when your hands were barely big enough to wrap around a shaft. I suppose to me you represented golfing purity. Youth. Instinct. The untutored, pure love of the game.

No one who loved the game like you, no one who can play like you, should be allowed to quit. That's a law, you know? And if it isn't, it should be.

I know your disease, son. Thank God it's mental, but then, in the final analysis, aren't all our diseases mental?

The ancient Hermetists had a principle, the First Principle they called it, that the universe itself was mental. They taught that All That Was existed purely as a thought in the Mind of God, or the All as they called it. Even we human beings with all our complexities had no substantial existence as matter, but were merely thoughts in the mind of our Creator, much like Micawber arising with his fellows from the mind of Dickens.

The Hermetists claimed you could change the universe, or your own at any rate, by transmuting it mentally.

Alchemy. Lead into gold. All in the mind.

Am I rambling on? Yes, I see your eye wandering. To what? Oh yes . . .

Go ahead. Take it down, it won't break.

It's not the original, you know. That, the holder is obliged to return to the Georgia G.A. after his year. This is a half-size replica that Jeannie had made up for me. It has a certain grace, I think. Lord knows it's the only thing I've ever won.

GEORGIA STATE GOLF ASSOCIATION

AMATEUR CHAMPIONSHIP

1946

WINNER

DR. HARDISON GREAVES

I'll confess a secret to you, Michael. Might as well, since before this night is over I will have bared to you the innermost holdings of my soul.

There were nights, after Jeannie died, when I would creep into this room, alone, in those black hours beyond the stroke of two, and steal a glance at that one word.

Winner.

Does that sound superficial? Perhaps it was a rather slender straw to grasp at. And yet there is something profound and mysterious about the vastness of the gulf between "winner" and "runner-up." Even one time, just once at any level, to *prevail*. To be, for one fragile moment, the best. It's not to be scoffed at,

Michael. It helped me to do it, and it helped me to witness it, one day long ago in 1931.

Yes, I know your illness, son. I'm going to try to cure it this evening with a story. Will you stay and listen?

It may take all night. I'll stay up if you will.

Good. Are you comfortable? That tea should be just about ready now. . . .

Two

I T SEEMS ODD NOW, but in the Twenties, business people and even a good number of families took their meals—not just lunch, but dinner and breakfast as well—at cafeterias.

Particularly in the South, these teeming emporia were the absolute rage. There were Burr's and Dawson's in Virginia and the Carolinas, Whistling Pig in Alabama and Mississippi, Roberdaux's, Tyrell House, and The Griddle. But the biggest and best of all was a chain called Invergordon's. There were five in Birmingham alone. Jackson had three or four, Nashville and Memphis the same. Richmond had ten.

Invergordon's were not the depressing impersonal factories that the word *cafeteria* evokes today. Each had a manager, usually a clean-scrubbed bachelor or widower, who lived on the premises in an immaculate suite upstairs. These mandarins prowled the tables dispensing goodwill and tending instantly to their customers' whims. One of them, a fellow named Adoor Moot, became Mayor of Charleston. That was how popular he was.

All the chains had hostesses, not just one at the door to seat the arriving guests, but a regular fleet of belles to serve the endless iced teas, Coca-Colas and coffees without which no Southerner could navigate from one end of a meal to the other. Invergordon Girls were the elite. They wouldn't deign even to speak to Burr's girls or Dawson's, so total was their disdain for these competing plebeian establishments. Invergordon Girls dressed in Scottish tartans and brought drinks, flatware and condiments with a smile and special twirl that they learned at the Invergordon finishing schools. Young boys would just gawk with their jaws slack, and girls couldn't wait to grow up and twirl at some newer and even more glamorous Invergordon's.

There was a Mr. Invergordon of course. A Scotsman from Sutherland, in the North Country by Dornoch Firth. A golfer.

Mr. Invergordon had money, buckets of it from his cafeterias and in the Twenties bales more from Wall Street. He wanted to build a golf course. Not just any golf course, but the grandest, most spectacular championship venue these shores had ever seen.

Remember, this was ten years before Augusta National. Other than Pinehurst, which was all but inaccessible geographically, the South lacked a true world-class layout. Invergordon set out to remedy that.

He owned twenty-five hundred acres of prime duneland off Wassaw Sound, east of Savannah. Linksland. There was a true sand beach on the south and east, and tidal flats on the mainland side that could be spanned by causeway. Drainage was excellent; there were snowy egrets, kites and petrels soaring in off the Atlantic. The breeze was fresh enough off the Point to keep the mosquitoes on their best behavior, not to mention give a round a smack of seaside interest.

Invergordon decided to build his links there.

He paid Alister Mackenzie $50,000 to design the course and oversee construction. I can't tell you what a fortune that was in those days. I don't believe Mackenzie earned half that for Augusta National and Cypress Point put together.

But Invergordon didn't stop at a championship layout. He brought in Charles Roy Whitney from Philadelphia to build a 500-room hotel, complete with physical culture pavilion, natatorium, an enclosed botanical garden, and artificial hot springs fired by underground steam furnaces.

He named it Krewe Island after his birthplace in Scotland.

For sheer scope and grandeur I would rank Krewe Island with the Hearst Ranch in California and the Vanderbilt estate in Asheville—and Krewe Island was, or would be upon completion, open to the public.

I know you're ahead of me, Michael. You've read of the Great Atlantic Storm of 1938. It was a hurricane, before they gave names to hurricanes. It blew for 54 straight hours with winds that hit 190 miles per hour. When it was over, Invergordon's dream was reduced to matchsticks.

The very land itself had been annihilated. The six outward holes that ran south along the Point were literally washed into the sea. There was nothing left. The last four, the home holes, with the exception of eighteen, were likewise obliterated. Everything was underwater and stayed that way for days. Salt water. When the sea finally withdrew, the South's most famous golf links was nothing but a salt marsh choked with debris.

Curious, and much remarked upon ever since, was the fact that the eighteenth hole was spared. It was actually playable the day after the storm. The green had drained, bunkers were dry, even the fairway had not a pinch of salt on it.

But I've gotten ahead of my story. For by the time this catastrophe struck, Invergordon himself was dead, and had been for almost nine years. Blew his brains out with a British Enfield .303 in his office on the top floor of the Cotton Mart in New Orleans. Crash of '29.

The Depression hit the South hard, and hit Invergordon's empire harder. Who could afford to eat out? Cafeterias withered where they stood. Invergordon's four sons didn't have the brains among them to make one decent businessman. It fell to Invergordon's socialite daughter, Adele, to salvage the family's fortunes.

Adele clung to Krewe Island, which at that point was still a year short of completion, perhaps believing as many did in the Crash's immediate aftermath that the dark times would soon pass, the economy right itself and money flow freely again. Or maybe just because she knew it was her father's jewel, the one creation that might outlive and even memorialize them all.

I remember, even as a boy, the desperation that suffused the ribbon-cutting ceremony. Krewe Island at last was christened.

She was grand, magnificent, spectacular. Not a single guest had slept a night on her virginal linen sheets, nor a golfer sunk his spikes into her immaculate bermuda fairways. And now it looked as if none ever would. The class of newly rich, the citizen millionaires, had been utterly wiped out by the Crash. All that remained of a possible Krewe Island clientele was the old rich and even they felt constrained, not so much by fear of the future as by an understandable reluctance to indulge themselves in luxury by the sea when so many of their countrymen were struggling so desperately just to survive.

Something had to be done.

Something to make Krewe Island transcend the current calamity. Something not just to lift it in the minds of the wealthy above the Greenbrier or the Homestead, but to make its extravagant existence palatable to the masses who would never be able to glimpse it, except in photos in the Society pages.

An event.

An occasion.

Something bold and dramatic, to capture the public imagination, lure the press, put Krewe Island before the eye of the world in a bright and even historic light. Money was no object, for if the Links and Hotel couldn't leap instantly into the black, the whole colossal enterprise was doomed.

Adele's brainstorm was this. A golf match. An exhibition for the unheard-of prize of $20,000. Between the two greatest golfers of the age, Bobby Jones and Walter Hagen.

Hagen the professional, if he won, would take the cash. If

Jones the amateur prevailed, the prize would be donated to the Atlanta Athletic Club.

The prospective contestants were approached and, for whatever reasons professional or personal, agreed.

A date was set.

And, true to Adele's dream, the story caught fire. Perhaps it was just what the country needed as it writhed in the tentacles of depression. A show. A circus. Something bright and patrician, on a sunny greensward by the sea, where two gallant knights would joust for a king's ransom.

Babe Ruth came down from New York by rail. Dempsey took an ocean view suite. Scott and Zelda flew to Savannah, motored daily to Krewe Island from her cousin's cottage on Poinsettia Street. Even Al Capone, rumor had it, was on his way to swell the gallery.

Savannah was beside itself with anticipation. The city tumbled headlong into the grip of madness.

Three

I WAS PRESENT for the next scene in this saga, but being ten years old and exhausted from a day of caddying, shagging and so forth was unfortunately sound asleep.

I must rely on the witness of my father, who had carried me along to the Hesperia Elementary School for the event. The Civic Auditorium would have been the appropriate venue for this colloquium, but that night was occupied by a Women's Christian Temperance meeting. The town fathers gathered at the nearest reasonable alternative. This turned into something of a fiasco, as the only chairs available for Savannah's loftiest personages were those designed for children aged eight and under. These were Lilliputian, to say the least. The dignitaries refused to sit upon them. They insisted on standing, which led, after five or six hours of heated, sweltering, smoke-choked debate, to a very real shortage of temper. But let me recall how my father told it:

It was Judge Neskaloosa River Anderson whose nose was out of joint from minute one. One of Invergordon's ditcher operators had accidentally shot the Judge's prize bitch, Jupiter. It wasn't so much the dog's death as the way Adele handled the apology; apparently she had no conception of how attached a Southerner could be to his best hunter. You could have shot the Judge's firstborn and it wouldn't have grieved him as much. Anyway, Old Neskaloosa took a stand opposing the golfing extravaganza, and his vote on the Council could put the bollocks to the whole damn shooting match.

The problem, as Judge Anderson saw it, was how much the city of Savannah was supposed to contribute to this exercise in private enterprise and greed. Our causeways would be used to transport spectators. Our streets would be employed for parking, our constabulary to maintain order, our homes to shelter the incoming hordes. Every office and business would be grievously inconvenienced for three days prior and God only knows how many days after. And the mess? Who would be responsible, who would clean it up, and most of all, who would pay for it? The judge felt that Adele Invergordon was taking advantage of Savannah's good nature. "Our city is the doormat," he declared, "upon which the heiress wipes her feet!"

At first no one took the old gentleman's protestations too seriously. There was a great deal of shouting and declaiming to the effect that this golfing match was the eco-

nomic boon the city was frantic for, that we desperately
needed it in these dire times. Hotel rooms would fill, res-
taurants be packed, the average citizen could charge for
parking, let rooms, perform services and in general line his
needy pockets off the visiting Goths, who, thank the Lord,
would in all probability be too-rich-for-their-own-good
Yankees.

But Anderson would not be swayed. The hours crawled
by and, as often happens when normally rational individuals
are too long cooped in an oppressive environment, the
seething throng began to transubstantiate into a mob. It
started coming over to the Judge's side.

If Adele Invergordon could offer $20,000 in prize money
to two damn visiting golf players, by God she could come
up with a matching sum for the civic coffers of Savannah,
in whose bosom and by whose sufferance this self-
aggrandizing stunt would take place!

A messenger was dispatched to Krewe Island and returned promptly with the heiress's refusal. I recall vividly
the phrases "adamantine in my resistance" and, more un-
fortunate, "blackmail."

Shouting and countershouting resumed with a fury. Savannah's pride had now been officially trodden upon. The
Judge's supporters swelled. The convocation divided into
two equally rabid bands: those who saw the golf match, and
the subsequent success of Krewe Island, as essential to Savannah's economic survival, and those who declared that

survival be damned, we had endured defeat in war with less of a blow to our honor and manhood!

The atmosphere was explosive. No matter how fevered the indignation at Adele Invergordon's affront to the city, all knew that the match must go on, Savannah was desperate for it economically. But how could it, now that our civic noses had been rubbed so ingloriously in the dirt? Cigar and cigarette smoke hung so thick you couldn't see from one side of the room to the other. Meanwhile many of the elders had yielded to gravity's demands and were perched absurdly on the kindergarten-sized chairs. The air was dense, humidity hovering just shy of out-and-out liquidity. Pools of perspiration pocked the hardwood floors, backs of shirts clung black with sweat. To this day I don't know whose voice finally called out the solution. What I do recall is the zeal and enthusiasm with which it was met.

The rafters shuddered with cheers; the little basketball backboards, only six feet high, nearly came off with the stomping of feet and clapping of backs.

Savannah would nominate its own champion golfer!

A *third* contestant, a local hero, to duel the great Jones and Hagen!

This was when, Hardy [my dad told me], you came to and began blinkingly to demand to know what was going on. The town solons were congratulating themselves furiously on this brainstorm that would save Savannah's name, draw attention to her fine young manhood, and so on, when someone—I suspect it may even have been myself—rose to ask whom precisely we would nominate for this loftiest of golfing honors.

Instantly the hall fell silent. A name was shouted. Dougal McDermott. Cheers burst forth, till the obvious was recalled: that McDermott was the professional at Krewe Island, an imported Scot who had barely set foot in the town except for a stiff snort or to chase down the local trollops. No, McDermott would never do.

Neither would Frank Laren, the pro at our pathetic Southside Public Links. Or Andy Dillion, the city champ. Or Nicholas "Nitro" Vitale, the greengrocer. There was one fabulous golfer, Enderby "Cottonmouth" Conyngham, whom all agreed possessed gargantuan length, immaculate course management and a lockpicker's touch around the greens. The only problem was Enderby was a Negro.

So desperate was the throng by this point that a debate of some ten minutes' duration ensued, in which half a dozen of the city's most fevered bigots, crackers and peckerwoods rallied to the black man's cause, frantic for a champion with a chance to prevail.

Then came the breakthrough.

"What about Rannulph Junah?" a voice cried from the rear.

"He's off to hell and gone, you damn fool! Tibet or Calcutta . . ."

"No, no—he's back! Been back a month."

Could this be true? Every heart leapt with hope. Rannulph Junah? Rannulph Junah!

Here at last was our man!

Scion of one of the South's wealthiest and most venerated families, triple letterman at Columbia, law review graduate of Emory in Atlanta, handsome as a god, brilliant as Apollo, Junah possessed every virtue of shining Southern manhood.

And he could play. My God, he could play.

He was long. Titanic off the tee, with a rolling draw that he could turn on and off like a faucet. He could cut the ball as effortlessly as he hooked it. He was the only man I ever saw who could make a spoon back up on a green.

He had won the Georgia Amateur at eighteen, the Trans-Miss at nineteen, and had reached the finals of the North-South in '27 despite a nearly ten-year hiatus from the game. The Walker Cup Committee had selected him as third alternate for the '28 squad, and he had even practiced with the team for a week at the Chicago Golf Club before withdrawing for "personal reasons."

Junah's iron play was fearless. He hit the kind of low screaming bullets that started out jackrabbit-high and rose like eagles to peak, tower, float till they were nearly motionless and then drop feather-soft to the green, where they would alight, as Sam Snead later used to say, like a butterfly with sore feet.

And Junah could putt. Eschewing the charging, hell-for-leather style then in vogue, he utilized a touch like gossamer to ghost the ball with aching, tremulous slowness up to the very marges of the hole, at which exquisitely tender gait it would topple in from any corner of the quadrant, and never lip out for excess of speed.

Rannulph Junah, Rannulph Junah, Rannulph Junah! The galleries rung with the hero's name. We must summon him, nay, collect him at once!

The crowd surged for the exits. But wait! The clock. It was nearly one in the morning! Manners precluded descending on the poor fellow at this hour, but, by God, the issue could not wait. A mad, sputtering paralysis gripped the posse. For an instant it seemed as if a mass nervous breakdown was immediately at hand. Then Willie "Argyle" Lofton, the town barber and sole Republican, spun straight toward you, Hardy. . . .

"The boy! Send the boy!"

This motion was adopted by instant acclamation, as various members of the congregation shouted out its virtues. You, young Hardy, knew Junah; you had shagged for him, caddied for him; Junah was partial to you. Send the boy to be sure our man was awake, to prepare him for the coming delegation (which would follow within fifteen minutes), but on no account, under no circumstances, divulge the nature of our call.

"Will ye do it, Hardy?" the throng queried as one.

"Well, I . . ."

That was all you got out, son, before half a hundred fevered hands seized you and began tossing you skyward in triumph like Mercury himself.

"Fly then, lad, with winged sandals on your feet!"

Four

THE AERIE, JUNAH'S PLANTATION, lay four miles down the Skidaway Road, backed up against the tide channels where my brother Garland and I used to paddle after porpoises playing with the shrimpers as they cut in and out for the fishing grounds. I rode the whole way on my Burke Lightning in under twenty minutes, despite ruts and washouts, no lights and a regular gauntlet of coon hounds and croppers' mutts that took after me at every fence line.

It got spookier out toward Junah's, for his property began nearly half a mile east of the gatehouse. There was nothing but weeds and pitch-black slough canals with pocket moccasins ghosting everywhere. I pedaled like hell and figured, Let 'em jump, I'll be where they ain't by the time they get there!

The closer I got to Junah's, the ghostlier it became. The big gate was rusty and untended, not a soul standing watch or a light anywhere. I was shocked at how rundown and gone to seed the place had become. The live-oak-lined drive was all ruts and weeds, dank as a swamp in the night dew with wet branches slapping against my bare legs under my shorts. I could feel cobwebs catch my face, and all manner of crawling things spring and fall on me.

Thank God there was a light ahead. Junah was awake! I pedaled up the stone drive. There was a Ford wagon parked out front, a Peugeot-Pickard sitting on blocks and a huge black Chalmers beneath the porte cochere. "Mr. Junah!" I hollered, more to hear my own voice for courage than expecting to raise him. "Mr. Junah, it's Hardy Greaves, come to hail you!"

No one answered for the longest time. I got off my bike and peeked in the big Georgian windows. The front hall was lighted, but by only a single flame on top of a piano. All the furniture was covered in ghosty white sheets.

Finally Ezra, Mr. Junah's main man, appeared in the side door and waved me over with a cross expression. "Master Hardy, what you doing out here this shade of night? You not hurt, are you?" I explained rapidly that my father knew of my whereabouts and in fact, along with the town elders, had dispatched me.

Ezra let me in, declaring he hadn't seen such urgency in no boy's eye since the day we whooped the Kaiser. "You sure Mr. Junah's awake?" I kept asking. "I hate to disturb him but I got to."

"Mr. Junah don't hardly never sleep no more," Ezra told me as we padded down underlit hallways. "The poor man is up all the night, just a-steaming and a-stewing."

We passed beautifully appointed rooms, all shrouded over in

sheets and dust covers. Where was Junah? I started getting scared all over again as Ezra led me outdoors, across another soaking stretch of grass.

We were headed back to the old slave quarters.

I trucked in after Ezra through a door so low even I had to stoop. Down a clammy stone corridor and there we were, stepping out into the ancient slave kitchen, a broad low-roofed room where the cooking had been done for fifty field men, maybe more. I blinked in the smoky dimness and then I saw Mr. Junah.

He was wearing a blue dungaree shirt, salty with sweat and open to the navel. His hair was long, over his ears, and hung unparted in glistening sheets in the lamplight. He wore clamming trousers, open to the knees, with no shoes. He was sitting at a hundred-year-old coarse-cut serving table with his crossed feet propped up and a long Kentucky cheroot between his teeth.

"Hardy, my boy! What a felicitous surprise! Come in and join us in a cold chicken sandwich!"

I was just a boy, and had glimpsed little if any of the darker grown-up world. But one thing even my innocent eyes could not fail to see. Mr. Junah was dead, stinking drunk.

Five

ADVANCED TENTATIVELY INTO THE GLOOM. Three or four colored men, apparently Junah's hands, sat and stood around the margins, faces and arms so black they seemed to blend into the ironwood walls.

"Gentlemen," Mr. Junah addressed them, his sun-burnished arm stretching elegantly to indicate me, "may I present the only male in Chatham County who isn't completely full of shit."

His hand clapped my shoulder warmly, I heard low chuckling from the darkness. I was frightened. I had never heard a gentleman utter such frightful profanity and had no idea what to make of it. Junah queried me as to whether my parents knew of my whereabouts at this hour and I blurted my nervous response. I could smell the liquor on Junah's breath. I began to tremble.

"Don't be afrighted, Hardy lad. Your host is far from inebriated. There's not enough whiskey in the state to get me as drunk as I need to be." He ordered a milk brought for me. One of the men fetched it from an ice chest against the far wall.

Then I realized Junah was not alone at the table.

At the far end sat a black man of about forty years, tall and striking, wearing threadbare suspendered trousers and a worn English-cut jacket. He was not drinking, but sat upright with impeccable posture, dark eyes like pools soaking up the lamplight.

Here was another shock to my untutored sight: a colored man sitting at the same table with a white. I must have gawked, or even started at the raw unholy cheek of it, because the man smiled and tipped his battered hat. I could feel my face flushing. The nerve of this fellow . . .

"You offered the boy a sandwich, Ran," the black man spoke. "Don't you think you should make good?"

Ran? Junah's first name. Worse, *short* for his first name.

The gall and effrontery were so egregious, my senses were struck numb. This was outrageous, unspeakable. Junah rose, steadied himself, then strode powerfully toward the black man. I braced myself for what certainly was coming: Junah's fist smashing into the brazen fellow's cheek, then Junah towering over his vanquished form, ordering the others to throw him out before he murdered him with his bare hands.

I was terrified, yet anticipating it deliciously. Would Junah break his neck? Actually kill him?

To my amazement, Junah strode straight past the black man, pausing only to brush an affectionate hand across his shoulder!

At the breadboard, Junah plucked a knife and plate and called back to ask if cold chicken or ham was to my taste!

"Forgive the tardy introductions, Master Greaves." Junah's gesture swept from me to the stranger.

"My mentor and boon companion, Mister Bagger Vance."

S ix

I HAVE PUZZLED FOR YEARS and lain awake many nights, trying to understand what it was about this mysterious fellow that held my attention so raptly. He did nothing whatever to put himself forward. When the elders arrived (which they soon did in a thunder of Reo, Hupmobile and Model A engines) and the drama decamped to its new setting in the library of the mansion house, Vance withdrew inobtrusively to a corner, where he took up a solemn post and stood absolutely still, observing with an utterly detached calm, saying nothing.

I couldn't stop staring at him.

Despite the high romance ensuing in the lights at the front, my glance kept returning, furtively I'm sure, to glimpse his powerful presence, which radiated some . . . I don't know what . . . some consciousness which I couldn't grasp or define but which I was certain was of utmost importance.

The best I can describe the effect the fellow produced upon

me is to say that that night, watching the way Vance watched, was the first time I had ever glimpsed my surroundings with something like objectivity.

Till then I had inhabited my boy's world as a fish inhabits the sea, taking it utterly as a given. As the only world that existed. The only possible world. Now for the first time I grasped the existence of this world *apart from myself*. Do you understand, Michael? Like a fish suddenly made aware that it is swimming in water, I found every aspect of my perception changed.

Not for long, of course. The drama up front was too compelling. There, by the grand piano, beneath the great wall of books, Judge Anderson was treading the boards like a tentshow revivalist. Invoking Savannah's pride, her chance to place a mark upon the consciousness of the nation, and so on. The elders (twelve, including my father) reinforced the Judge like a phalanx of Pharisees. Before these, Junah stood, listening patiently with a wry twist on his handsome features. I saw his hand raised for respite, the Judge ignoring it, Junah smiling, lowering his eyes, then announcing in a soft but clear voice that there was no possibility that he would participate in the golf match.

The elders didn't hear.

Or if they did, the words slipped past in a willed blast of disbelief and denial. "Of course you will," Judge Anderson continued without hesitation. "Now: have you the proper clubs and equipment?"

"I said I won't play," Junah repeated softly.

"Don't trifle on a matter of such import." Anderson began losing patience.

"Please don't make me repeat myself," Junah said. "I do not wish to participate. My decision is final."

The Judge's face went plum-red. The man beside my father staggered, faint. Several of the others stiffened, seemed poised to step forward and actually thrash Junah. Others simply gaped in disbelief. As for myself, you could have scraped me off the floor with a spatula.

"You cannot be serious, sir," my father addressed Junah. "The city must have a champion, and no one but yourself is worthy."

"I'm sorry, Doctor. I have given up the game."

Blank silence. I could see my father steady the man beside him, who now appeared close to a coronary. "When I was a child, I spake as a child," Junah said, "but now I put away childish things." His voice was soft with sorrow. "Besides, I've lost my swing."

"Oh, balls and nonsense!" Anderson thundered. "No one 'loses' a swing, and if you have, by God, you've got seventy-two hours to find it!"

A chorus of assent seconded the Judge. The elders surged forward, swamping Junah. I could hear his voice proffering the names of other candidates, the ones previously suggested at the town meeting, who he declared would uphold the city's honor every bit as well as he.

"Balls again!" Judge Anderson's voice boomed. "We don't

need some damn sawed-off Scotsman or some local pea-shooting pipsqueak to be pooping drives forty yards in Jones' and Hagen's wake. We need a man with thunder in his fist. A hero, to boom that pill out past these golfing gods, to make galleries gasp and journalists rend their thesauruses seeking new adjectives of wonder! We need a knight, sir, and that can only be you!"

Junah remained unmoved. I could no longer see him, he was so surrounded in the crush, but I could hear my father's voice, speaking calmly, trying to restore reason. He knew, my father said, that Junah had suffered greatly during the War and afterward. The city was aware, however dimly, of Junah's wanderings over the globe, his quest for some redefinition of meaning in his life. . . .

At this point, unable to see and not at all clear on what in the world my father was talking about, my eye lit upon the writing desk beside me. Here were scribblings, a journal of some sort, apparently in Junah's own hand.

Odd-looking volumes spread across the desktop. Titles that meant nothing to my boyish eyes, though in later years I came actually to inherit these same books. *Sartor Resartus, The Way of Chuang-tzu*, the *Kybalion, Life of Paracelsus*. Some texts were in Chinese or Japanese, others in Sanskrit or Arabic or Hebrew or Farsi, alien tongues that I couldn't even begin to guess at but that I knew no God-fearing Christian would have a dime's worth to do with; and then, in the center of them all, scrolling obscenely from the center binding of some Hindu text, was a color illustration of such pornographic intensity that I literally feared for my soul, just for having glimpsed it. Its image burned into my brain no matter how tightly I shut my eyes: scores of snakily intertwined bodies, writhing in a mass of elbows, knees, nipples, buttocks and lips to form some kind of pan-erotic architectural column that looked like nothing quite so much as the bottom of a bait can. And this, it was clear, was something religious! Poor Junah. The man had clearly taken leave of his sanity.

It was then that I became aware of Bagger Vance's presence beside me. I could smell him. He had come over in the crush, apparently deliberately. I looked up at his towering form, the veined muscles of his arms, his thick sinewy wrists. His hands gently closed the book, refolding the illustration. He smiled an inscrutable smile. The odor that came off him was not like that of other black men, or other field men white or black. It was deeper, more pungent. It reeked of Life, of the earth, of something wild and pure, like an unbroken horse or a wild elk, and yet at the same time it went beyond animal, into something consummately human and complex. I was held as if by a spell. My sense was that he could have killed me in an instant, snapped my neck like a wishbone or crushed my skull with one hand, and yet, inexplicably, what came from him was a sense like what the Hindus call *ahimsa*. Harmlessness. In the intentional sense. Not that he couldn't harm, but that he wouldn't. In fact he would protect.

I realized that he liked me. In a flash I liked him too.

Up front, the mob was backing before Junah's now-impatient surge. He was telling them no, and no again. "I'm sorry, gentlemen. I wish you luck in securing the champion you seek but I must repeat, with finality, that it will not be me."

The crowd rocked rearward; they believed him now; for the first time, true despair began to grip the assembly. I could feel Vance's hand nudge me gently.

"If I may speak, sir," Vance's voice broke the silence, addressing Junah.

"We don't need any more damn coffee!" Judge Anderson roared at the interruption. All eyes spun toward Vance, thinking him one of Junah's servants, and a damn fool one at that.

"Go ahead, Bagger," Junah said gently.

"I was thinking, sir, of our discussions." Vance spoke to Junah, stepping forward to stand beside the desk with the volumes and writings. "Do you recall what we spoke of, regarding entering the spirit by way of the flesh?"

"I do," replied Junah.

The elders stared, baffled and dumbstruck.

"I was thinking," Bagger Vance continued, "that if you'll change your mind and play, I'll be happy to carry your clubs."

A laugh burst from Junah.

"You? You'd be my caddie?"

"I'd consider it an honor."

Every eye in the room now wheeled from Vance to Junah. No one knew what the hell to make of this mysterious black man, who he was or what sway he held over Junah. All they knew was Junah was listening, Junah's refusal was wavering.

Judge Anderson swept forward, seizing the moment to step beside Vance, who in seconds had vaulted from the gutter to the jurist's most lofty esteem.

"What do you say, sir?" Anderson addressed Junah. "The man, by God, is talking sense."

Seven

J UNAH WAS IN.

Hagen and Jones would arrive the day after tomorrow; there would be a practice round that afternoon, banquets at Krewe Island in the evening, then the actual match the day after. Seventy-two hours to marshal an operation on the scale of the siege of Vicksburg.

The city's madness expanded exponentially. Special trains had to be added, then more and more after that, to handle the multitudes arriving, not just for the match but to serve those arriving for the match. In those days, Michael, the wealthy didn't travel on their own, lugging their carry-on bags through airports and heading to Hertz for a rental car. They traveled with entourages, all of whom needed rooms and food and towels and hot water. Now entourages were arriving to serve the entourages. Freelance cars and drivers flooded in from Atlanta, Columbia, Mobile; men hired themselves

out as chauffeurs, footmen, guides, bodyguards, porters and bell-
men. Waiters and chambermaids poured in; every able-bodied man,
woman and boy was pressed into service. I remember my friend
Billy Utaw's mom's cook, Addie, being chosen by lot to be cham-
bermaid for the suite that Bobby Jones would share with O. B.
Keeler. It was like they'd all just been called to the head of the line
for heaven. Billy's head swelled so you couldn't talk to him, and his
mom began putting on airs like the Queen of Sheba.

My brother Garland was out all that first night cornering the
market in grape snowball syrup. I myself was held down almost
literally by my mother, who insisted that I get my sleep before I
took sick and ruined my own and her chances to take advantage
of this once-in-a-lifetime opportunity. I would never have for-
given her except that, that morning, I encountered greatness for
the first time face-to-face.

Arnold Langer took a room with us.

Mother had agreed finally to allow some of the descending lo-
custs, as she called them, to stay under our roof. She refused
however to accept compensation, insisting on giving the space,
plus breakfast, dinner and supper, as a pure gesture of hospital-
ity. One thing she insisted upon, however: that her home would
not be open to mere rubbernecking tourists, but only to working
people with a legitimate purpose for being in Savannah. As luck
would have it, that included journalists. Sportswriters.

Langer covered sports for the *Atlanta Constitution*. My dad had
taught my brother and me to read by poring over the great word-
smith's columns. Langer came with a friend from Boston, a
former classmate from Harvard who was an actual book writer;

they took over both spare rooms upstairs as office space, plus Garland's room which he vacated, moving in with me.

It was barely nine in the morning when their cab arrived from the station, and they were already lathered in sweat, their white shirts sticking to their undershirts, which were wringing wet beneath their wool jackets. They stunk of cigarette smoke and sweat and pure literary glamour. Both of them chain-smoked and coughed and hacked and when I carried their coats up to Garland's room which would now be theirs, I felt the weight of whiskey flasks in the pockets.

Sitting to breakfast, Langer's friend asked for his eggs soft-boiled, the first time I had ever seen eggs cooked any way but scrambled or sunnyside up. I watched mesmerized as he set a steaming uncracked egg upright in its little porcelain cup, rapped it sidewise with a butter knife to knock its crown off, then spooned the gooey innards right from the shell, to vanish with a worldly slurp beneath his mustache. It was the most glamorous sight my eyes had ever beheld.

Over coffee, the journalists regaled my mother with tales of Jones and Hagen. How Jones never traveled to a tournament without his friend and Boswell, O. B. Keeler, who was a newspaperman himself, covering sports for the *Atlanta Journal*, and a true scholar of science and history, almost mystical in his study and appreciation of the game. Jones, in fact, gave Keeler half the credit for the 1930 Grand Slam and insisted when posing with all four trophies (and the Walker Cup, which the Jones-captained team had won that same year) on Keeler's standing beside him as an equal.

Hagen traveled with a staff of five, headed by his caddie-cum-valet Spec Hammond, whose responsibility it was to supervise the shining of the Haig's thirty-eight pairs of shoes and the pressing of his seventy pairs of slacks and plus fours. Hagen habituated the Savoy in London, dined on oysters and champagne for breakfast, and never had his hair cut except by his own personal barber from the Detroit Athletic Club, whom he either flew personally to visit or had flown in, worldwide, at his own expense.

In the cool of the screened rear patio, Langer lit a Chesterfield and began to turn the subject toward Junah.

Did we know of Junah's exploits in the Great War? That he was a bona fide hero? Of course, my mother replied; our city had produced numerous men of valor, and certainly no less could be expected of a man of Junah's background and breeding. Langer smiled as my mother recited the names of Junah's forebears and their heroism at Antietam and the Wilderness, Shiloh and Bermuda Hundred. Langer acknowledged appreciatively the South's long record of bravery and the fine fighting men she had produced. But, he said, he had never heard a story quite like Junah's. Did we know what happened to him in the Battle of the Argonne Forest, and how he reacted afterward? Langer's memory was fresh because he had looked up the accounts and dispatches in the news files before leaving Atlanta. He thought they might somehow work in to the reports he would file on the coming match.

My mother declared that she—all of us in the city, in fact—were familiar with aspects of those wartime events, but the full picture remained rather mysterious and unclear. Something about a French wife who died and Junah's daughter, now being raised by *grand-mère* in France.

The journalist corrected her: it was a German wife. And a queer story behind it.

It seems Junah, at some desperate point during the battle, faced with being imminently overrun by the enemy, had called in artillery fire on his own position. He and one machine gunner were the only two still alive, cut off from their unit, behind their single gun whose barrel had actually warped from the furious fire it had put forth. They were in fact overrun, Junah and his gunner surviving only after a desperate hand-to-hand struggle with bayonets and entrenching tools. Junah himself was gravely wounded and required nearly two years in the hospital, in England and the States, to recover.

Junah's heroism involved killing eleven Germans in this encounter; they were found dead around his position when the attack ended. He and his gunner were awarded the Medal of Honor, which Junah, for himself, refused to accept. His brigade commander was compelled to claim it for him, with Junah intractable in his hospital bed.

After the armistice, Langer continued, Junah was transferred stateside to a veterans hospital in upstate New York. Upon his release in 1920, he chose not to return to Savannah, or even to remain in America, but took ship immediately for Germany. There, in the ruins of that shattered nation, he sought out all eleven families of the soldiers he had killed. Most had suffered terribly. Some rebuffed him, some slammed doors in his face, others broke down and embraced him with appreciation for his gesture and his courage.

"Of all things," Langer addressed my mother, "Junah wound up marrying the sister of one of the soldiers he had slain. Apparently they were very much in love, had a daughter within a year, and were planning on returning to the States. Then Junah's bride herself died tragically in an outbreak of typhus. It's not clear exactly what happened with Captain Junah over the next several years. Apparently this final death was more than he could bear. Something broke inside him. He turned over his infant daughter to the care of her Bavarian grandmother and vanished into that seething ferment that was postwar Europe. Reports placed him in Paris for a time, among expatriate artists and writers, then traveling by ship, working his way it seems. He was in the East, India, Ceylon, the Himalayas. He returned briefly to Savannah in '27, as you know, and tried to pick up the threads of a normal life, even campaigning with some success on the amateur golf circuit. But this attempt apparently failed to quell his restless questing. He set out again two years ago, traveling, reading, studying, seeking heaven only knows what.

"Throughout these peregrinations, Captain Junah, it seems, has been accompanied by a mysterious servant who, though technically in Junah's employ, is said to exercise tremendous influence over him. The fellow appears and reappears at random intervals; no one knows when or where he and Junah first became acquainted, or even the man's name. . . ."

"You mean Bagger Vance!" I blurted. "He's here now. He's caddying for Mr. Junah in the match!"

Both Langer and his friend reacted with instant interest. "You mean the fellow really exists," Langer queried, "and is still in Junah's employ?"

I confirmed this with vehemence. "Heck, if it wasn't for him, Mr. Junah wouldn't even be playing tomorrow! When I got out to his house last night, he was dead drunk. Two in the morning and couldn't hardly stand. . . ."

I became aware of my mother clearing her throat rather dramatically. Both scribes' eyes were wide open now, bony shoulders thrusting forward like vultures. I saw at once my faux pas. My mother's hands were tugging me from my chair, explaining to my interrogators that her son must study (even though school had been let out for the rest of the week) and how they, as experienced interviewers and journalists, must know never to put credence in a young boy's tales, which are so notoriously exaggerated. Langer, ignoring this, was just framing his next question when the screen door banged open and the day was saved by my brother Garland, bursting excitedly in.

"Get your shoes on, boy! Jones and Hagen, they come in early!"

"What? How . . ." I stammered.

"They're sneaking in on an early train, to duck the crowds. Come on now or we'll miss 'em sure!"

With my mother pushing, we bolted straight outside, smack into the Messner twins' dad's hired man Albert whose ancient Ford stakebed was creaking by with a load of green melons. Garland shouted to him if he'd give us a scoot to the station. Albert laughed and told us they already was about sixteen million folks jammed in there, packing the streets and spilt over onto every porch, stoop and rooftop. "Y'all boys won't see jack squat a-racin' there. Climb on the truck with me, for the motorcade."

"What motorcade?"

"Don't y'all know nothing? The motorcade out to Krewe Island!"

Eight

TO UNDERSTAND BOBBY JONES' STATURE in the South at that time, you have to remember that the War of Northern Aggression (as we called it in our family), or Civil War as the Yankees preferred, had by no means then receded into the benign past. Its memory was fresh as a still-open wound. Not so much the war itself, for the South had achieved abundant glory on the battlefield, nor even the fact of defeat, for in surrender the nation yet maintained a certain grim dignity. It was that obscene and lingering hell euphemistically labeled Reconstruction that rent the Southland's soul and ground her honor into the dirt.

As recently as the 1870s, private property was still being confiscated under the Domestic Reparations Act. My own grandfather had all his weapons, including two antique shotguns and a Tennessee long rifle forcibly taken from his house by Federal officers in '79. I still recall the cold rage of that proud gentleman when he spoke of the helplessness and despair he endured in that moment. Families were still being put off the land in the 1880s, and the poor agrarian Negro, who of all was most blameless, was still being exploited by that element of shameless Northern locust known as the carpetbagger.

Then must come the admission that in each Southerner's private heart, even the most ignorant cracker and peckerwood's, lay hidden the dishonorable truth that our side, however valiant its champions, however noble its defense of sacred home soil, was the side that stood in line with human slavery and fought for its preservation.

This secret knowledge of our collective guilt, which none but the most courageous would give thought, let alone voice to, lent an added agony to our nation's vanquishment and prostration. My father said many times that the wonder wasn't that the South expressed so much rage, as that she expressed so little. Compare her to Weimar Germany, after its mortification at Compiègne.

It was that same pain, the loss of national manhood, that the South felt so keenly. Not just the men, whose culture had been built on a beau ideal of manly pride and virtue, but the women, children and servants whose psychological security depended upon the stability and power of their fathers, brothers and sons.

The Great War helped. The heroics of Southern warriors like Alvin York of Tennessee and General Black Jack Pershing. But even their spectacular exploits were performed beneath the stars and stripes of the hated Yankee flag. As late as the 1920s, the South had not produced a champion with the combined virtues of spectacular achievement and Southern purity.

Not until Robert Tyre Jones, Jr., of Atlanta.

Permit me, Michael, passing over his scores of lesser triumphs, to recall only the major championships Jones collected over a brief seven years.

1923	U.S. Open
1924	U.S. Amateur
1925	U.S. Amateur
1926	British Open, U.S. Open
1927	British Open, U.S. Amateur
1928	U.S. Amateur
1929	U.S. Open
1930	British Amateur, British Open, U.S. Open, U.S. Amateur

In that brilliant span, Jones won 13 of the 21 national championships he entered. He won all three of the British Opens he played in and one of the two British Amateurs. In nine U.S. Opens from '22 to '30 he finished first four times and second four times. So dominant was he in his prime that the two professional titans of the day, Walter Hagen and Gene Sarazen, never won an Open championship, in Britain or America, in which Jones was also entered.

Bobby crowned this incomparable stretch, surely the most glorious ever in American sport, with the Grand Slam of 1930. He retired from competitive golf then at the pinnacle, at age twenty-eight.

I remember the city of Savannah, and no doubt the entire

South, glued to the radio broadcast of the ticker-tape parade down Broadway, when Bobby returned from Britain with the first two legs of the Grand Slam. You could hear the cheers and the music, the harsh Yankee voices of the broadcasters describing the scene. Then the microphone was placed before Jones. Over the air came that soft Georgia accent. My father had to turn his face away to hide his emotion. My mother wept openly.

Here at last was our Grail Knight, our Parsifal. Jones' triumphs, the very fact of his existence, seemed all by themselves to recall the South from decades of ignominy and exile. His graciousness, his gentility, the fact that he was not a coarse Northern striver but a gentle-born chevalier, an amateur. Jones embodied the finest qualities of Southern manhood and he had not just whipped the Yankees but the whole damn world.

And now here he was. In our city. Crossing the causeways in an open car toward our own Krewe Island. From our perch atop Albert's watermelon truck, my brother and I could see the glistening wetlands extending ahead for half a dozen miles and, rising out of them by the sea, the towers of Krewe Island's grand hotel. It was a pilgrimage. The motorcade stretched a hundred cars ahead and hundreds more behind; Model A's and Plymouths, Reos and Auburns and Packards, crawling, sputtering, backfiring from their sizzling-hot, trembling exhausts. Farmers' wagons choked the route. Autos would overheat and stall and be pushed out of the way by the onswarming pilgrims, sometimes straight into the wetland muck, like casualties being shouldered aside by an advancing army.

Hagen was up there beside Bobby, suntanned so dark he

looked wood-stained, grinning to the girls and favoring the ma-
trons with a little cavalier gesture of his hat. Flowers were being
tossed into the open back of the car. Bystanders pressed apples
and pears on the heros. "Bobby! Bobby!" they cried, even the
barefoot swampers for whom golf, or the idea of sport period,
was as alien as some notion from the moon.

Bobby was their knight too. He had crossed the ocean to take
on the world's best and come home bearing not just their silver
cups, but their admiration and respect as well.

Jones stood on a par with the other titans of the decade—
Lindbergh, Dempsey, Tilden, Ruth—and, in the eyes of many,
surpassed them all.

But where was Junah?

Had anyone contacted him? Did he even know that Jones and
Hagen had arrived? Would he miss the practice round? I
strained my eyes in every direction but saw no sign of the Ford
or the Chalmers.

At Krewe Island, the scene broke down into pure merry bedlam. Cars parked anywhere they could, on fairways, levees, raw
gooey muck; a mass surge swept Hagen and Jones on toward the
hotel and the tented pavilion that had been erected outside. Garland and I wriggled forward, worming our way through the
crowd. With a leap and a hand from Judge Anderson, we were
home free. Up there! On the podium.

There must have been fifty reporters, plus every political scal-
awag for 500 miles, all jostling for position in front of the cam-
eras. Adele Invergordon was up front, looking glamorous and
mouthing words of welcome which were utterly lost in the feed-

back and echo of the microphones sputtering for power. It took almost ten minutes for something resembling order, not to mention electrical current, to arrive, and Garland and I used every second to wriggle our way closer. I was scuffling with one meaty fellow, right up near the mikes. He stepped on my foot, just about breaking my toes; I turned to curse him and saw his huge suntanned hands. It was Hagen.

He squeezed through, up to the mikes, just as Adele Invergordon finished introducing Bobby. I couldn't take my eyes off Hagen's suntan. It was the darkest, most glistening and flawless I had ever seen. Even the crinkles around his eyes were bronze. This was in the days, remember, when men did everything to stay out of the sun. Hats were universal, collars high; to see a man bareheaded outdoors was a rarity and being tanned or burned was a sign of low station, of one whom necessity forced to labor in the heat of the sun.

Yet on Hagen, that tan shone like a badge of honor. It evoked sun-drenched fairways and Côte d'Azur beaches, deck chairs on the *France* and champagne at concours d'elegance. Every kid within eyeshot vowed instantly to spend each future second in the sun, till he too had achieved that godlike luster.

The Haig was thirty-eight then, with his name engraved on the trophies of nearly a dozen major championships, a seasoned master at the peak of his maturity and power. More exciting still was his arrogance, his cocksure self-confidence. He radiated a roguish swashbuckling deviltry, which made him even more a brilliant match for the gentle knight Jones.

But it was Bobby who was speaking now before the mikes.

From the far side, at last we saw Junah arriving amid an escort of troopers with Bagger Vance striding powerfully beside him. They made their way swiftly through the crush, Vance helping Junah ascend to the platform, then himself withdrawing among the crowd. Jones noted Junah's arrival with a cordial nod, gesturing for the others on the podium to clear a space. A reporter called out, "Sir! Mr. Jones!" It was Arnold Langer, just below Bobby in the crush.

"You've been quoted as stating that golf is actually three different games. Golf, tournament golf and major championship golf. In which category, sir, would you place this match?"

Jones smiled and the throng chuckled with him. It was a good question.

"There is always one measure by which any match can be evaluated. That is the skill and courage of one's opponents. When a man's foes are worthy, every match is at championship level."

Hagen grinned broadly and made a little impromptu bow. The crowd roared with affection and approval.

"My worthy adversary here, for example." Jones gestured not to Hagen, but to Junah. "I've never actually had the pleasure of competing head-to-head with Mr. Junah, but he and Jess Sweetser did skin five dollars from myself and Watts Gunn in a practice round before the '28 Walker Cup." A surge of laughter and applause from the throng. "I don't believe Mr. Junah missed a putt under ten feet all day—and certainly not when there was money to be made!"

The crowd roared with delight and appreciation. Many of them, no doubt virtually all of the out-of-town arrivals, had never heard of Junah and almost certainly regarded his inclusion in this event as a rather embarrassing sop to local pride. Now they relented somewhat in this harsh appraisal. It was Jones' doing, deliberately, being the gentleman he was, to include Junah and set him in the light of a credible opponent.

On Junah's face could be seen acknowledgment and gratitude for this gesture. Yet still his emotion, if a word must be given to it, was mortification. He seemed self-conscious and uncomfortable, standing there as the cheers of the locals rang around him and Jones' smiling gesture turned to the other side of the platform. To Hagen.

"As for this fellow"—Jones' soft accent reverberated through the loudspeakers—"whose name for the moment escapes me . . ."

Deafening laughter and applause. Hagen beamed. Jones had won the crowd utterly. With a modest wave (you could see he relished the act of public speaking not at all), he stepped back and turned the microphone over to Hagen.

A fresh surge of enthusiasm swept through the crowd as the Haig came forward. He was wearing gray plus fours with matching argyle socks and the type of two-tone shoe we used to call "spectators." His linen shirt was white, with a dove-gray tie the precise hue of his plus fours. Everyone else was wringing and sopped. Hagen's shirt betrayed not a smack of sweat.

"It is indeed an honor," Hagen spoke slowly and clearly into the mikes, "to compete against a man whom many consider to be the greatest ever to pick up a club. A man not only blessed with matinee-idol good looks and animal magnetism, but also one of the truly fine gentlemen of the era. But enough about *me*. . . ."

The crowd roared. Jones was laughing with genuine enthusiasm, I could see Keeler rocking appreciatively and nodding his head.

Hagen, it should be remembered, of all the knights who ever strode the fairways, ranks behind only Jones and Jack Nicklaus in number of major championships won. Eleven in all, ahead of Hogan, Snead, Palmer, Watson, ahead of all save the two greatest ever. The Haig took the U.S. Open at Midlothian in 1914 and at Brae Burn in '19. He captured the British four times, at Royal St. George's twice, in '22 and '28, at Hoylake in '24 and one final time at Muirfield, 1929.

Then there was the PGA, which was held at match play in those years. Hagen transformed this championship into his own private fiefdom, winning first in '21, then four times in a row, '24, '25, '26, '27.

Then there was that royal shellacking he gave Jones in their first head-to-head exhibition match in Florida. The fans hadn't forgotten it and neither, the bet was sure, had Bobby.

As I watched that brilliant pair up front on the podium, a thought, or more precisely an emotion, struck me then with a power that has not left in all these years.

I had the profound sense of these two, Jones and Hagen (and even Keeler in an odd way), as being *something other than mortal*. They seemed a breed beyond. A finer, higher order of being. Creatures who inhabited a nobler, loftier plane than we mundane humans; beings bordering on, and perhaps at times crossing over into, being gods.

I looked at Hagen, beaming with his glowing dark skin and brilliantined hair, holding the multitude enthralled with his power and magnetism. You could understand how this man had defeated 22 opponents in a row, 22 of the finest players in the world, over four consecutive PGA championships, all of which he had won. It was a function not so much, one felt, of his skill as a player, as of his power as a competitor. He was daunting, intimidating, overwhelming.

I turned next to Jones. There are two things that photographs, and even films of him, never quite depict. First was his athleticism. Even at his modest height and size, even with the air of intelligence and gentlemanliness he projected, even in his shirt and tie when he seemed more a figure for a veranda than an arena, he exuded a youth and strength that were frightening. His shoulders underneath his cotton shirt were broad and powerful; he stood like a supple god. There was something almost Greek about him, and yet at the same time consummately American.

Then there was his handsomeness. You've no doubt seen numerous photos of the man, Michael, perhaps even some of this very day at Krewe Island. But none do justice to the man that stood before the multitude in his youth and prime. My God, he was handsome! His skin, like Hagen's, seemed to glow with an inner fire that the rest of us had been denied. His eyes were bright with power and intelligence and his whole modest understated demeanor only added to what I must call, for no other word will accurately describe it, his beauty. Almost unaware of it, vaguely embarrassed by it, never dreaming of capitalizing on it. If it makes sense, I may say his good looks were "amateur." Do you know what I mean?

The terrifying thought occurred to me, as perhaps it did simultaneously to the whole crowd, or at least our local Georgia half of it, that these two titans would utterly trample and annihilate our homegrown knight. A chill coursed through me. I knew I must turn next to Junah, but I was afraid to. Afraid that after the glow and power of Hagen and Jones, that my eyes would settle on our local champion and find him a mere mortal. I had to force myself, force my eyes to swing and focus on Junah, whom I could sense now moving to the microphones. I heard his voice before I could make myself actually look.

"Now I know what a sacrificial lamb feels like."

I opened my eyes . . . and Junah held up! Thank God! A wave of relief flooded through me at the same time the crowd's enthusiastic laughter swept upward to the podium. Junah too had that look. That look of power and athleticism, the capability, one sensed, of rising to levels beyond the mortal. He too seemed cut from that same transcendent cloth.

The whole crowd must have been silently thinking the same thing, for at that moment an audible "Ahhh" seemed to expel from a thousand throats. In that instant, the people of Savannah took Junah to their hearts. He became in that instant their champion, and all their hopes attached themselves with joy to his fate.

"So be it"—Junah gestured toward Hagen and Jones—"lead me on to the slaughter," and the crowd inundated him and the platform with their heartfelt cheers.

Right behind Garland and me stood Judge Anderson, the man whose prideful insistence had forced Junah into this match and onto this stage. "Was I wrong?" his voice boomed triumphantly to several of the elders who had at first opposed him. "No," admitted his foes, vanquished.

Junah melted back, away from the microphone, as the cheers redoubled in anticipation of the upcoming practice round. I had one brief moment to glimpse his face, before dozens of swarming bodies intervened, and what I saw confused and chilled me.

Not warmed whatever by the applause, Junah's expression seemed more than ever to be one of distance and despair. Dark clouds lowered upon him. I glanced into the crowd and saw Bagger Vance, watching just as he had that first night, with utter detached objectivity. Then he too was swallowed by the throng.

N i n e

THAT AFTERNOON PASSED as the most excruciating hell I had ever experienced in my young boy's life. It was torment at its purest, for I was dispatched onto the course, supposedly in a position of responsibility and honor, yet that very position kept me just out of range of seeing the players and the round. I missed everything.

Do you know what a forecaddie is, Michael? I didn't, until I found myself in the tumult following the welcoming ceremonies being swept up by two of Dougal McDermott's assistant professionals and whisked with seven other boys, amid much urgency and excitement, into Krewe Island's staff locker area. There tailors were waiting to fit us (and scores of other marshals, officials and gallery guards) with navy-blue plus fours, white linen shirts with the Krewe Island monogram, and matching navy neckties. It was clear this was a great honor; my inclusion was apparently in deference to my father's position in the community, and also a reward for my own work of the night before. It meant nothing to me; all I wanted was to be with Junah and Bagger Vance.

How could I get out of this and back to them?

I caught McDermott by the jacket sleeve and blurted some incoherent barrage of excuses: I had schoolwork, a sudden fever, dizzy spells. But he took it all as boyish nervousness and, loudly for the other forecaddies as well, refused to hear of it. "Ye'll all remimber this day as long as ye live!" He clapped my back, and steered me back among my fellows. We were each given two flags, one white and one red, four feet high with a sharpened steel point at the bottom. Our job was to make sure no ball got lost.

McDermott issued us our marching orders. In teams of four, we were to leapfrog one hole ahead of the match. A pair of us would be stationed in the landing area on each driving hole, one to the right of the fairway, one to the left. We were to follow each ball in flight and, should it land in any place where it wasn't immediately visible, in the heathery rough or beyond among the duneland, plant our flag right beside it—white if the ball was in bounds, red if out. Another pair of boys were stationed around the green to mark any wayward approaches, while the second quartet, to avoid getting gummed up in the galleries, moved on ahead and took up positions at the next hole.

The result was the most exquisite torture a golf-mad boy could be forced to endure. I could see Hagen, see Jones, see Junah, but only as miniature figures 275 yards distant, indistinguishable one from another until they swung, and most of the time virtually invisible in their white shirts and light-colored plus fours against the background of the gallery in identical attire. You could see a player swing, recognize Hagen by his lurching motion or Jones by his slow, stately tempo; then all your focus had to switch to the ball, which you were obliged to scamper under, tracking it like some relentless outfielder till it hit and rolled safely to rest in the officials' view. That was all you could see or were allowed to see. You couldn't see the players' faces, couldn't see their swings nor their grips, their footwork, their rhythm. You couldn't hear the jokes they cracked or watch the emotions play across their faces. As soon as you staked your flag and made certain that the marshals had the balls' positions clearly in view, you were obliged to scoot away, not even to the green where you might still catch a glimpse of the excitement, but an entire hole ahead.

To make the ordeal even more painful, it was clear that players and gallery were having great fun. The competitors all hit more than one ball, sometimes two and three off each tee, drawing and fading. We forecaddies could look back from a hole ahead and see Jones dropping a ball in the rough for practice to get the feel of the grass, drop another fifty yards behind his drive to rip a long iron into a green and see how it held, or drop two or three close in for niblick pitches and run-ups. They all hit practice shots from fairway bunkers and around the greens chipped from two or three angles. From the deep distance I could see them putting, three or four balls from various levels on the greens, at all probable pin positions. For one stretch of three holes, the eighth through the tenth, Hagen played on ahead, alone, taking just Spec Hammond his caddie and his gallery. He had us running crazy with our flags because he, apparently deliberately, was hitting his drives into trouble, left and right, just to practice playing out. I lost track of Junah and Jones entirely, and when Hagen rejoined the group at the eleventh, Junah was gone.

What catastrophe had struck now?

I peered back down the fairways to see if Junah had dropped a hole or two behind to practice alone. Had he pulled a muscle? Cut his hand? Where was he? Had he dropped out completely?

When we got in, near sunset, I found Garland and learned that Junah had returned to the practice area after the turn, hit a handful of desultory pitches and sand shots, then departed without explanation, with Bagger Vance driving the Chalmers, for home.

I was getting frantic. I had no idea what private darkness Junah was struggling with, but the image of his face two nights ago in the slave kitchen, that bright desperate smile over his whiskey, and then the blank despair on his features this afternoon made my blood run cold. In some unspoken way, I had identified my own fate with Junah's. He was my champion as well as Savannah's. The thought of some desperate debacle, some ghastly mind-driven collapse before the world's eyes, was so awful I couldn't bear even to contemplate it. And yet I felt it coming. Sensed it in my bones, even if I had no idea why or from where.

It was evening now; the banquets had begun in the east and west ballrooms. We boys could hear the orchestra music coming from across the broad lawn, see the gay formal lanterns lining the drive and the queues of automobiles delivering their cargo of ladies and gentlemen at the brilliantly lit entrance of Krewe Island's grand hotel. We ourselves were feted to a fried chicken, brunswick stew and peach cobbler supper in the employees' dining room. A dormitory had been set up in a carriage house for the forecaddies and the cooks and others, so we wouldn't have to fight traffic tomorrow.

I had to get out of there. Had to get to Junah's and beg him to include me somehow in his outfit tomorrow; I'd carry ice or sandwiches, anything to get close and be able to see. The thought of passing that day, potentially the most memorable of my life, exiled into the blue distance, an entire hole ahead of my idols, was more than I could bear. I got to a phone and called my brother Garland, who was already fevered with envy over the forecaddie uniforms with the Krewe Island monograms and the fitted plus fours. Would he take my place tomorrow? Hell yeah! I told him where I'd stash the stuff once I snuck away and he promised to collect it; he'd sneak out tonight and creep in with the forecaddies before dawn. Krewe Island had even fitted us for a brand-new pair of shoes, real spiked spectators that we'd be given at breakfast. Garland could have those too.

Back in bed I feigned sleep for what seemed like hours. My bunkmates chattered and giggled, wide awake with excitement for the morning, while out in the hall the chaperone and dorm master drank coffee and flirted with various chambermaids passing. Midnight came and went; no one had corked off or looked likely to. I gave up and crept to the lavatory, shinned down out the window and beat it away across the lawn. The banquets were starting to wind down, you could see tuxedoed men and bejeweled women stealing kisses out by the cars and in the little alcoves with the statues along the covered walks. Some fool was splashing around in the main fountain, singing a song with dirty words while a flock of Marcel-waved girls cheered him on, giggling. I ducked back through a service entrance and into the pastry kitchen. A couple of cooks were smoking by the big scullery sink, talking about how Jones had gone to bed at the stroke of ten, while Hagen supposedly had no plans to sleep at all. The cooks seemed in that good-natured state of work exhaustion so I let them see me. What about Junah? I asked. Did they know if he'd come in for the banquets? They started laughing like I'd said the funniest thing in the world.

"Come in? Hell, he's drunk half the liquor from the second and third services!"

I don't know what inspired me to ask this next, but from my mouth came "What about his caddie? Was he with him?"

"If you mean that strange-ass dark sumbitch, he was in here not twenty minutes ago, getting ice." They pointed out the hallway where Bagger Vance had gone.

I took off in pursuit. Down one carpeted corridor that yielded nothing, then following my instincts down another and another. Loud music was coming from several rooms up ahead, doors were open, I felt like I was getting warmer. I turned into a fourth corridor; a crowd of plastered party-goers pushed past, hooting and grabbing at each other. The hall was a mess. There were half-empty wine goblets and ice pitchers set on hors d'oeuvre trays that had been pillaged down to the platters. A lit cigarette was burning on the carpet. A woman ran out of one room and into another without a top, laughing, cupping her hands over her breasts, and then two men came after her, not laughing, huffing and puffing in dead earnest. I turned a corner and glimpsed a dark form way down the hall. Bagger Vance? I raced off down the carpet, a good forty yards, and when I tore around the corner, something slick took my feet wildly from under me; I flew sideways slam-bam into a wall and crashed like a load onto the floor. Golf balls! Half a dozen were scattered across the carpet, with a whiskey glass set on its side like a target.

Someone had been putting. My eyes just had time to spot the blade setting against the wall, a Victor East putter exactly like Junah's "Safecracker," and then a sound like a cry came from the room straight across. I peered in and there in the darkness was Junah, half naked on the bed, with two women pawing and grinding all over him.

I don't believe I had ever beheld a grown woman's buttocks before. Certainly I had never witnessed that peculiar swiveling, gyrating motion or heard those urgent, throat-catching gasps. Junah was half out of his tux, with the one girl on top of him and the other kissing him from the side, while his hands switched back and forth between both of them. He didn't see me, none of them did, their eyeballs were rolled back so far into the sockets. There were empty whiskey bottles on the carpet; the whole room stunk of alcohol and cigarettes. I had never witnessed a scene so degrading or so utterly devoid of dignity. Part of me wanted to throw up; another wanted to charge in and give all three of them the thrashing they so richly deserved. I stood there, dumbstruck and paralyzed, when a quiet voice spoke from behind me.

"Don't think too unkindly of him for this."

I spun. Bagger Vance stood there. Taller even than I remembered and cold solid sober, with that same poise and gravity radiating from him so powerfully. He put a hand on my shoulder and gave an odd smile. "Think you can handle that big persimmon in there?" His gesture indicated Junah's oversized deepfaced driver, leaning against a chair just inside the room. "Grab it and the putter, we've got work to do."

Vance said nothing more, simply turned, scooped the balls from the carpet and strode toward the service exit. I grabbed the driver and sprung after him, out the door and across a rear grass parking area. Bagger Vance strode powerfully ahead, past the last parked car and buggy and on out into the dark dripping duneland. I looked back; the lights and music from the ballrooms were dropping farther and farther into the distance, we were out there in the night with nothing but the dunes and the raw black sky. "Where in the world are we going?" I gasped, breathless, when I finally caught up.

Vance turned off the sand, onto a narrow track that led to an open fairway. "To walk the course," he said.

Ten

I T WAS PAST ONE O'CLOCK and by no means warm. The wind cut sharp and damp off the Atlantic, making me shiver. "You're cold," Bagger Vance said. "No, I like it," I told him. He smiled and again put a hand on my shoulder. Immediately I was glowing like a furnace. Even when he took his hand away, the flush remained, coursing powerfully through the bloodstream, warming me to my toes! "How did you do that?"

"Stop here," he said, indicating a level spot on the first fairway. "Let me see you take a stride."

It was becoming clear that Bagger Vance never answered a question directly. He always diverted you, or changed the subject, and yet you felt that he *was* answering somehow, in some delayed-action elliptical style of his own.

I took a few strides under his critical eye. A little longer, he directed . . . shorter now, that's it. One stride equals one yard.

We began pacing off yardage. From the middle of the second tee to carry the fairway bunker on the right: 243 yards. From the hummock fronting the sixth green to the upper level of the green itself: 41 yards. Vance took it all in. As I strode off, earnestly pacing some yardage he had directed, he would linger in a green-side bunker, wriggling his soles down into the sand to sense the firmness; then, as he raked the area flat, nodding to himself as he filed the information away. He kept it all in his head, no notes. On the seventh and ninth greens, he had me putt balls across the various quadrants, up this slope, across that hogback, while he absorbed their wet-spinning paths in the dew. "The grain will shift tomorrow as the blades of grass follow the sun." His hand traced an arc east-to-west in the sky. "The same green will break differently in the afternoon than in the morning."

At the ninth green he knelt thoughtfully, gliding his fingertips across the nappy grass. "They'll mow the back nine late, probably only a half-dozen holes ahead of us, then remow all the greens between eighteens at lunch. Keep that in mind, Hagen and Jones will."

We strode swiftly through ten, eleven and twelve (apparently Vance felt he could get a sufficient sense of them just from a quick look) and were just commencing the six inward holes when I saw him pull up and squint back behind us. A man was coming. I could make out a white shirt and jacket, with the moon rising behind him. Oh hell. "What is it, a marshal? Should we run?"

"Look again," Bagger Vance corrected me. "Can you see who it is?"

The man was two hundred yards off; an owl with cat's eyes couldn't have recognized him. "It's Mr. Jones' friend," Bagger Vance spoke, "Mr. Keeler."

Sure enough, it was O. B. Keeler. He came toward us in his necktie and spectacles, peering with a certain apprehension at first, then relaxing, apparently with recognition, as he got closer. "I'm relieved to learn I'm not the only lunatic out here at this hour."

He was walking the course too. With a pedometer on his hip and a notepad in his pocket. He came up to Bagger Vance and held out his hand. "I'm O. B. Keeler. You're Mr. Junah's caddie, aren't you?"

Vance introduced himself and me. There was a bit of polite talk about yardages. Keeler felt you could never trust them as indicated on the card. "No one ever actually paces them or puts the transit to them. The architect eyeballs them once on a flying visit and that's what you're stuck with!" He chuckled to himself. "You can't go to school on your opponent's bag either. Tomorrow Sir Walter'll hit full mashies 140 yards and choked lofters 150, as if no one's caught onto that trick." Keeler was clearly a patrician, scholarly fellow; I was certain he would excuse himself quickly from a colored man and a boy. To my surprise he didn't. Instead he sighed, folded his arms across his jacket and peered out thoughtfully over the duneland.

"A golf course is a different place at night, don't you think? I've walked a thousand of them. Some revert to nature the second the sun sets. They lose their identity as products of man. Deer graze on the fairways and bunkers seem absurdly artificial."

He glanced at Vance; then, satisfied that he was being seriously listened to, continued. "Then there are other courses, the great ones I've found, that remain themselves even under a foot of snow, their character is stamped so strongly upon them."

"Which class would you place Krewe Island in?" Bagger Vance asked.

The faintest flicker crossed Keeler's face, a shadow of surprise at the depth and intelligence in this soft-spoken caddie's voice. "This is an odd one," Keeler answered after a pause. "My sense of it is more like a battlefield than a golf links. Can you feel it? The presence of ghosts. I've had the same feeling at Shiloh, walking among the stones of the dead." He shivered, as if to shake off some unwonted apprehension. "And yet the course herself is a beauty. I'd rank her in the world's top ten already, and she'll only get better as she matures."

Keeler finished. A kind of loneliness seemed to come from him, standing there in the chill. "Would you like to walk along with us?" Bagger Vance said.

"It would be my pleasure," Keeler answered with genuine warmth.

He and Bagger Vance walked on, talking. I missed most of what they said over the next two holes because Vance had me off pacing yardages. They were talking about the swing and chuckling. You could see Keeler still didn't know what to make of this self-effacing yet obviously extremely intelligent caddie. On the fifteenth tee, they were waiting when I scurried back with the yardage from a fairway bunker.

"Let's see you take a cut." Bagger Vance held out Junah's driver to me.

"You mean hit one?"

"Just give us a few swings."

They had apparently been discussing some theory, and I was to be their guinea pig. I didn't mind. I took the big deep-faced driver that Junah called Schenectady Slim, planted my feet and gave it a wail from my soles. Once more, Bagger Vance requested. I swung again. When I looked up, he and Keeler were both chuckling merrily.

I felt like a fool, half ready to slam the club down and storm off, when Bagger Vance again caught my shoulder with that warm strong hand. "We're not laughing at you, Hardy," he said.

"No," Keeler followed, "more at our own poor selves, I fear." Keeler explained, "We chuckled out of envy, envy of youth and fearlessness." He declared that if he had torqued his spine through half the turn I had just taken, it would put him in the hospital for a week.

He spoke thoughtfully for a few moments about a boy's natural swing, any boy's. The big raw pivot, enormous arc, the natural sense of balance, release and turn.

"May I take it, sir," Bagger Vance said when Keeler had finished, "that you believe there is such a thing as the Authentic Swing?"

You could see Keeler cover his astonishment. Apparently Bagger Vance had hit on something Keeler *had* thought about, and was deeply interested in. "The Authentic Swing, did you say? Yes, I do."

He looked at Bagger Vance deeply, solemnly, still more than a little amazed to be addressed so seriously and with such intelligence by this odd, mysterious man.

"Tell me, sir, if you wouldn't mind," Keeler said, "what are your thoughts on it?"

Eleven

"**H**AVE YOU EVER SEEN identical twins take up golf? Their swings from the very first are radically different. Isn't that odd?"

Keeler absorbed this from Vance, nodding thoughtfully. Yes, he had seen twins swing. Yes, how interesting that their motions were so different. . . .

"Or," Bagger Vance continued, "have you ever watched a boy pick up a club for the first time and swing? I mean his first swing ever. And then seen him years later as an accomplished player? Isn't his mature swing virtually identical to the one he took the first time he picked up a club?"

"That is so," Keeler agreed enthusiastically. "Please continue."

"Or consider a professional instructor trying to alter a student's swing to fit some preconception of the proper motion. It's virtually impossible, is it not?"

Keeler agreed. "I see you're driving at a point, sir."

Vance paused. Keeler stood, absolutely attentive. "I believe that each of us possesses, inside ourselves," Bagger Vance began, "one true Authentic Swing that is ours alone. It is folly to try to teach us another, or mold us to some ideal version of the perfect swing. Each player possesses only that one swing that he was born with, that swing which existed within him before he ever picked up a club. Like the statue of David, our Authentic Swing already exists, concealed within the stone, so to speak."

Keeler broke in with excitement. "Then our task as golfers, according to this line of thought . . ."

". . . is simply to chip away all that is inauthentic, allowing our Authentic Swing to emerge in its purity."

We had reached the sixteenth green. Keeler paced beside Vance as he strode the putting surface, examining its slope and grain. "That's why a boyhood swing like your young friend's here is so fascinating. We marvel at its raw purity and unselfconsciousness. It's why we laughed involuntarily when we saw it. It shamed us, in a way."

"Think of a swing like Hagen's," Bagger Vance resumed. "That lurching slashing motion, could you teach that to anyone else? Could anyone other than Hagen even make contact with the ball? And yet for him, it's perfect. It is authentic. It is he. The swing he was born with, the swing that is the true expression of his existence.

"Have you noticed, Mr. Keeler, the endless praise and even adulation that is heaped upon your friend Mr. Jones' swing? To watch it evokes emotion, does it not? One might even say love; and do you know why? Is it not because we, in some deep intuitive part of ourselves, recognize Jones' swing as Authentic? The pure expression of his being, his inner grace and nobility, his power, his concentration and even his flaws and imperfections? Jones' swing embodies every aspect of his being like a perfect poem or symphony, and, if I may guess, has embodied it from the start."

Keeler assented emphatically. "I believe you're on to something, sir! I've known Bobby since he was thirteen and, do you know, his swing today is virtually identical to the one he possessed then and, I'll wager, to the swing he had at ten and eight and even six. Probably the first swing Bobby ever took would be recognizable to us, had we film of it."

"And before that," Bagger Vance declared. "Before he ever picked up a club. Before he was even born."

Vance paused, realizing that Keeler had a notepad in his hand. "Do you mind if I take some of this down?" Keeler asked. Bagger Vance hesitated, but continued.

"Consider the swing itself," he said. "Its existence metaphysically, I mean. It has no objective reality of its own, no existence at all save when our bodies create it, and yet who can deny that it exists, independently of our bodies, as if on another plane of reality."

"Am I hearing you right, sir?" Keeler asked. "Are you equating the swing with the soul, the Authentic Soul?"

"I prefer the word *Self*," Bagger Vance said. "The Authentic Self. I believe this is the reason for the endless fascination of golf. The game is a metaphor for the soul's search for its true ground and identity."

"Self-realization, you mean?"

"If you like. We enter onto this material plane, as Wordsworth said, 'not in utter nakedness, but trailing clouds of glory do we come from God, who is our home.' In other words, already possessing a highly refined and individuated soul. Our job here is to recall that soul and become it. To form a union with it, a *yoga* as they say in India."

"You've been to India, sir?"

"Many times," Bagger Vance replied. "In the East, men are not embarrassed to speak openly of the Self. But here in the West, such piety makes people uncomfortable. That is where golf comes in.

"The search for the Authentic Swing is a parallel to the search for the Self. We as golfers pursue that elusive essence our entire lives. What hooks us about the game is that it gives us glimpses. Glimpses of our Authentic Swing, like a mystic being granted a vision of the face of God. All we need is to experience it once—one mid-iron screaming like a bullet toward the flag, one driver flushed down the middle—and we're enslaved forever. We feel with absolute certainty that if we could only swing like that all the time, we would be our best selves, our true selves, our Authentic Selves. That's why we lionize men like Hagen and Jones and treat them like gods. They *are* gods in that sense, the sense that they have found their Authentic Selves, at least within the realm of golf."

Keeler was now utterly in Vance's thrall. We had passed off the sixteenth green and were climbing the rise to the seventeenth tee. Ahead we could see the ballroom lights and hear the orchestra music, faint scraps of it coming to us on the air. "Tell me, Mr. Vance. How does one find, if that's the correct word . . . how does one find his own Authentic Swing?"

"I will answer that, Mr. Keeler. But before I begin, let me make an important distinction. The wild fearless cut we saw young Hardy take a few holes ago, that was *not* the Authentic Swing. It is a precursor, a foreshadowing. To reach the Authentic Swing, a player must pass through three distinct stages.

"First the pure state of unconsciousness, or preconsciousness. Pre–self-consciousness. This is the state in which our youthful companion resides now. He doesn't think about what he's doing, he simply picks up the club and swings. This demonstrates deep wisdom, because it expresses faith in the existence of the Swing, it launches itself fearlessly into the Void. Unfortunately this pure state, like youth itself, cannot last. It must by Nature's law pass on to the next stage."

"Self-awareness"—Keeler strode step-for-step beside Bagger Vance up the rise—"self-consciousness."

"Exactly," Vance acknowledged. "In this stage, we realize that we possess an Authentic Swing, but we can't repeat it. Some days we can't find it at all. Our frustration mounts. We begin to study, to seek instruction, to strive by dint of effort to mold and control our motion. This as every golfer knows leads only to despair. We cannot overcome golf by force of will."

Vance stopped at the pinnacle of the teeing ground for the seventeenth. He looked out pensively over the dark duneland that stretched for a thousand yards along the night shore. His focus seemed to have wandered, to have left Keeler and traveled to some distant shore in his mind.

"You said there was a third stage," Keeler prompted. "A stage, one assumes, beyond self-awareness."

"Few reach that level, as we well know." Bagger Vance smiled, returning from whatever inner land he had journeyed to. "And then only briefly. It is as elusive as Enlightenment. Merely to realize we possess it makes it fly from us. And yet paradoxically it is always there, nearest of the near, closer to us than our own skin."

"But how," Keeler pressed, "how do we get to it?"

"It gets to us," Bagger Vance said. "Surrendering to it at last, we allow it to possess us."

"The Self, you mean?"

"And then we can play."

A soft chiming sound interrupted us. Keeler tugged a silver railroadman's watch from his vest pocket. It chimed its last sweet beat. "My goodness, it's four A.M. I must get at least an hour of sleep." He was torn, you could see, wanting to stay up and listen to Vance all night.

"Sir, could you briefly, as we walk in, expound on this subject just a little more? Is there a path, a Way, that leads us to the Authentic Swing?"

"There are three," Bagger Vance said.

Unfortunately I missed most of what he said, for he had me

pacing yardages on these two last and most important holes. I scooted out quickly, with Vance shouting after me not to rush but to keep my strides uniform, then scurried back as fast as I could while still being true to the yardage. I confess that a part of me was distracted, held spellbound by the grandeur and majesty of these two spectacular closing holes—"Prudence," number seventeen, a 444-yard par four, uphill and awesome in the moonlight, and eighteen, "Valor," which tracked the phosphorescent surf for 541 grueling brilliant yards. In a state of near rapture I caught what I could of the instruction Vance gave to Mr. Keeler.

The first path, I heard him say, was that of Discipline. It had something to do with beating balls, with endless practice, an utter relentless commitment to achieving physical mastery of the game.

Second was the path of Wisdom. I heard practically nothing of what Vance said here (I was checking yardage to three separate bunkers off the eighteenth) except, I believe, that the process was largely mental—a study of the swing much like a scientist might undertake: analysis, dissection, and so on.

Third (and this I heard most of) was the path of Love.

On this path, Vance said, we learn the Swing the way a child acquires its native tongue. We absorb it through pure love of the game. This is how boys and girls learn, intuitively, through their pores, by total devotion and immersion. Without technically "studying" the swing, they imbibe it by osmosis, from watching accomplished players and from sensing it within their own bones.

"All three of these paths embody one unifying principle," Vance said. We were now approaching the eighteenth green.

"That of surrender. Surrender of the Little Mind to the Big Mind, surrender of the personal ego to the greater wisdom of the Self.

"The path of beating balls defeats the player, as it must, until he surrenders at last and allows his swing to swing itself. The path of study and dissection leads only to paralysis, until the player likewise surrenders and allows his overloaded brain to set down its burden, till in empty purity it remembers how to swing.

"In other words, the first and second ways both lead to the third. Love is the greatest of these ways. For in the end, grace comes from God, from the Authentic Self. But to plumb this mystery would take us far more than a night and, I'm sorry to see, we have reached the final green. You must be very tired, Mr. Keeler."

On the contrary Keeler was energized, electric. "I won't sleep a wink after this," he said, "but I suppose I must try." He extended his hand. "Mr. Vance, it has been my good fortune to encounter, and I may say to interrogate, many of the most profound thinkers on the game alive today. You, sir, tower above them all. We must meet again and continue. It would be my fondest wish to have you discuss these thoughts with Bob."

"I have," Vance declared cryptically. When Keeler reacted with surprise and inquired eagerly to know when, Bagger Vance evaded the question in his usual pleasant but firm manner, remarking only "Before you met him."

They took their leave at the eighteenth, Keeler striding off vivid with energy, squinting to read his notes by the late moon. Across the dunes, the orchestra had finally retired; at last the shoreline slumbered. I looked up at Vance, who had resumed his distant expression, gazing out again over the silent linksland. For many moments he remained in this pose, motionless and rapt. Some thought or resolution seemed to crystallize inside him; I could see him return to the present and become again aware of me, still in attendance beside him.

"Mr. Keeler's instincts are truer than he thinks," Bagger Vance spoke quietly, once again placing that warm powerful hand on my shoulder. "A battle *was* fought here, once, long ago." I followed his hand as it swept across the rolling dunes, indicating a plain along the shore and including, it seemed, a vast expanse out over the water.

"In the days when the austral constellations hung visible in this Northern sky, before the Great Ice retreated to the pole, this ocean we call Atlantic withdrew as far as the Afric shore and gave birth to a brilliant continent, a land called Mu. Its peoples were mighty warriors, artists and magicians whose knowledge of the subtle powers far surpasses anything our so-called moderns possess today."

His hand indicated the land from the seventeenth, back down to the twelfth, then stretched out over the water, which apparently had been dry land then. "There, where you see, great armies once clashed in battle lines that stretched as far as the horizon. Blows thundered heavenward, steel upon steel, and horses and men cried out in victory and death." He paused. "That was nearly one *yuga* . . . twenty-one thousand years ago."

It sounded, of course, completely fantastic. And yet I believed him. "How do you know all this?" I asked.

"I was there," Bagger Vance answered casually, as if it were the most obvious thing in the world.

He looked down at me, to see if I believed him. I felt the power of his eyes, their warmth and even love for me. I was held as if by the sun.

"Junah was with me as well," he smiled, still touching my shoulder. "And do you know what, young Hardy? You were there too."

Twelve

I WOKE UP LYING IN THE BACK SEAT of the Chalmers with a pillow under my head and a blanket on top of me. Light was in my eyes and Bagger Vance was shaking my shoulder.

"Wake up, young man, it's almost six. Time to get your breakfast."

I crawled out, blinking. Spectators' cars were already arriving; you could see their headlights in the foggy dawn, creeping down the lanes already packed on both sides with parked automobiles.

People had slept in their cars, camped out right on the road-sides. Men were scratching their hindsides and pissing off into the cattails. An enormous kitchen tent had been set up on the rise inland from the hotel; sweet coffee and egg smells climbed from the stove flues that protruded from its bright arcing canvas. Latrine tents rose from the various parking areas; bleary-eyed galleryites were already forming lines.

Vance wiped my face and poured me into a clean shirt and

long trousers, which he had brought along apparently for just this purpose. He gave me a two-quart steel jug and a rucksack-type pack, canvas lined with rubber. "Go to the employees' kitchen, use this badge if they give you any trouble." He handed me an official Krewe Island I.D., dove-gray with plum letters: COMPETITOR. (Vance wore one too, pinned to his caddie's cap.) "Fill the jug with hot sweet tea. Put ice in the rubber pack, plenty of it, and nestle five crisp apples among the frozen blocks. Put a couple of bananas in the main pouch pocket and as many raisins and nuts as you can fit in the others." He straightened my shirt and smoothed the hair out of my eyes. "Make sure you get a good meal in your own belly first. And empty your bowels before you start for the course!"

"Where are *you* going?" I turned back as he scooted me on my way.

"Meet me at the practice tee in an hour. I must wake Junah."

The carriage-house dorm was bedlam when I got there, looking for Garland. Men were trying to shave, peering over each other, five to each mirror, while the sounds of farting, pissing, coughing, spitting and hacking echoed like a TB ward. Every man was smoking already, and many of the boys. "Thirty-six holes today, lads," Dougal McDermott was calling, already dressed and shaved, with a steaming mug of coffee in his fist. "Tee-off at eight sharp and no excuses!"

I found Garland out in the tent kitchen. He was with the other forecaddies, dressed in shirt, tie and plus fours with his flags beside him at the table; they were all wolfing down chipped beef on toast and glowing like princes. Garland declared me a fool for giving up such an opportunity, and vowed he wouldn't switch back no matter how much I begged him. Then he tugged me aside and swore me to secrecy. "You'll never guess what I saw, in the locker room not ten minutes ago. Swear to me on your soul, cross your heart Mama 'n' Daddy never part, or I'll never tell you." The other forecaddies protested; Garland had apparently already told them the secret, which they now considered their own private treasure. "He's my brother, dammit, and I'm gon tell him." Garland glared. He ordered me to cross my heart and spit. I did. He tugged me closer.

"I was washing up, back yonder in the dormitory, and my bladder was about to bust. The stalls were all full, so I went outside; I was about to let her go right there in the bushes, but ladies kept passing on their way to the dining room. I thought I was about to pee in my brand-new pants. Then I saw an attendant duck through to the players' locker room; the door was open so I scooted in after and flashed off fast so he didn't see me.

"My, it was grand in there, Hardy, all carpeted and quiet with only three bags standing by themselves up against the wall, with the heads of their irons all emery-buffed and shiny, the woods all a-gleaming, and two sets of spit-polished shoes beside of each bag and little handwritten cards, all neat and perfect, saying 'Mr. Jones,' 'Mr. Hagen' and 'Mr. Junah.' I thought about swiping them little cards, they must be worth jillions, but just then I heard that attendant or something coming, so I snookered into the back and there I was, in the shiniest damn shithouse you ever saw. You could eat your supper right off the floor, I swear, that's how clean she was. There was Kreml hair tonic and Vitalis up there on the shelf, all free, just help yourself, and witch hazel and rubbing alcohol and cotton balls, and even combs and tooth powder, and each commode had a pure mahogany wood seat. Hell, I figured, I ain't gon waste this by only pissing, I'm gon drop a full load, just for the glory of it.

"There I was, a-perched on this brand-new commode that probably nobody's ass hadn't never sat down on, when I heard fast footsteps, spikes a-clattering, coming in to the sinks. The stall door banged open two down from me and I heard this god-awful retching, puking, disgusting sound. I zipped up and peered under the stalls. There was a man down there on his knees, with his hands on the rim of the bowl; the poor bastard was just heaving his guts up right into the commode! I froze right there on my bowl, with my feet tucked up so he wouldn't see me. I could hear him finish and flush and then wash his mouth out in the sink and spit and heave some more, splashing Listerine around to kill the smell and even swallowing it. I raised up, tiptoe on the commode seat, so I could just peek over the top rim of the stall. The man's hair was all hanging down in his face, I couldn't make out who it was. Then he combed it back and leaned forward into the mirror and you know who it was?" Garland paused dramatically, peering around to make sure no one could overhear. "It was Walter Hagen, bigger'n shit!"

"You're a damn liar!" I shot at once.

"If I'm lying I'm dying!" Garland grabbed me by the shirt-front and pulled me tight to him, shook me hard so I'd know he meant it. "Hagen was so cat-nervous he couldn't even hold down his breakfast. I know cause I looked after he left, and there was eggs and toast bits in that stall, sprayed over on the seat and the floor too."

This was more than I could endure. "Now I *know* you're lying, Garland. The Haig never eats nothing for breakfast but oysters and French champagne!"

Garland's lip curled, he released me. "Believe what you want, son, but these eyes know what they seen. It was Walter Hagen and he was puking his damn guts up."

I staggered back, reeling. Tawdry Jones, one of the other forecaddies, caught me by the shirtback. "Breathe a word of this ever and your ass is sweet green grass."

The sun was full up now; already you could feel the heat steaming from the earth. It was nearly seven. The grounds before the hotel were packed with spectators emerging from the dining room and others arriving from the main drive. I filled my jug with hot tea as Bagger Vance had instructed me, and collected the apples and bananas and nuts.

Out by the press tent a bunch of reporters and spectators were clustered around a ruggedly handsome older man they called Grant. It was Grantland Rice, I learned later, and he was answering a question, holding forth like royalty.

"The seduction of golf? I'll tell you its root. It goes back to the time before we were born, when we orbited in the ether, bodiless and without form. Don't write this down, boys, I'm using it for my own column, maybe even for a book!"

The reporters laughed and kept scribbling.

"In those precarnate days, our consciousness existed much as it does now in dreams. That which we willed or imagined, our minds created instantaneously. A city. A shoe. A solar system. We had only to think and it appeared, complete to the tiniest detail.

"Then, alas," Rice continued, "we took upon ourselves the travail and torment of physical existence. We were born. We acquired a body. All memory was lost of that perfect bliss in the prenatal firmament. Or was it? Nay, we sought now, without suspecting its mystical source, to recapture if only for a moment the sensation we had known in the womb of the stars. We sought to think *and to make our thoughts so!*

"I've lived and breathed sports my whole life and, mark me, this is the power by which they hold us spellbound. They remind us, when we perform an athletic feat aright or even vicariously, when we witness others doing so, of our days before birth. Our days in the ether. To throw a blistering fastball and watch the leathern pellet streak swift as thought precisely where we willed it: we feel like gods! We have willed, and our will has made it happen. To rifle a perfect pass. To fire the perfect punch. To pound a perfect serve. All these recall that idyllic existence, traces of which still linger in memory below the surface of consciousness.

"But tell me, gentlemen, and I will yield to any man who can gainsay me: is there another field of athletic endeavor upon which man can work his will that is grander or of greater scale than a golfing links?

"The distances alone! Out here we may visualize a drive of 300 yards, by God nearly three times as far as the mightiest home run, and then we execute it! And not just distance but accuracy as well. Consider a screaming long iron that rises and banks, fading or drawing exactly as we imagined, 210 yards to land precisely on target and stop within inches of the hole. From an eighth of a mile away! *That* is godlike! It makes us feel our will triumphant, we return to that paradise in which we dwelt before our natal hour.

"Why quibble that this taste of perfection comes only once in a hundred shots, or once in a thousand? We taste the nectar once and must ever after continue to seek it.

"That glimpse, gentlemen. That glimpse the goddess of golf grants us when she will, and that is all she requires to render us abject before her forever!"

The reporters laughed and surrounded Rice, kidding him good-naturedly. "That may be the reason on the ethereal plane," one spoke up loud, "but down here what brings 'em out is a plain old head-knocking. They come to see battle. To see a man spill another man's blood."

Jones and Keeler were already there on the practice tee when I hurried up at five minutes before seven. There must have been two hundred spectators already, held back by ropes and swelling three and four deep just to watch Jones hit his warm-up shots. I had the apples and ice now and resettled them so the pack wouldn't leak.

Behind the crowd I could see the Chalmers pull in, with two police cycles rumbling ahead as escorts. The spectators stirred and jostled and there came Junah, stepping forth tall and handsome as the gallery parted before him. Bagger Vance emerged behind, carrying Junah's bag. Photographers set up for photos. Junah obliged graciously but without pleasure. I saw Jones wink over and Junah smile back.

On the practice tee, which was clipped as short and flawless as a putting surface, waited three pyramids of golf balls, brand-new high-compression Spalding balatas that were so white in the sun you couldn't look at them without squinting. Jones could see that Junah was shy about approaching him, so he came over on his own, smiling, with O. B. Keeler, and they shook hands and wished each other luck. I was fetching the shag bag from the Chalmers and couldn't get back quickly enough in the swell to hear what they were saying. I could just see them talking, two knights of the fairway, both tanned and athletic and handsome in their immaculate linen shirts and perfectly creased plus fours. Apparently Keeler had told Jones about last night on the course, and about Bagger Vance's theories. Keeler beside Jones was gesturing to Vance, motioning him to join their group. Vance declined with a diffident motion of his hand, apparently thinking it unseemly for a caddie to fraternize with his golfing superiors. Keeler insisted, and reluctantly Vance came over. I got there just after the introductions to find Jones regarding the tall and still self-effacing caddie thoughtfully. "Are you sure we've met?" he asked, studying Bagger Vance's features. "I'm certain I would recall a face as striking as yours."

"It was a long time ago, sir," Vance answered softly. There was a pause. Something about the way Vance said it. You could see Jones puzzling, studying Vance as if for a meaning beneath the surface.

"It's all I can do to remember yesterday." Junah stepped in, dispelling the tension in laughter. Vance seized the chance and withdrew subtly, easing Junah to the fore. The group crossed to Jones' pile of practice balls; photographers clustered; Jones began lobbing easy pitches down to his shag boy. He chatted with Junah and Keeler in between shots, nipping each pitch perfectly with his flawless languid rhythm, nudging each successive ball from the clutch with his clubhead, positioning it precisely at the back edge of the previous divot. "Every warm-up session is a new adventure, isn't it, Mr. Junah?" he remarked in his soft Georgia drawl. "One never knows which swing he'll find that morning, or if he'll find one at all."

Junah chuckled. "I haven't found mine in five years." You could see he and Jones were both battling nervousness, each seeking to establish a solid controllable rhythm for themselves for the day.

"I'm certain your caddie can help you," Keeler put in with a smile, trying to draw Bagger Vance closer into the circle. "If anyone knows how the swing is learned, I'll wager it's he."

There was a pause. "The swing is never learned," Bagger Vance said softly. "It's remembered."

Jones' clubhead was just positioning a fresh ball. He stopped abruptly. The Grand Slam champion looked up, studying Vance's face with a deep thoughtfulness.

"You were right, O.B.," he said with a grin to Keeler. "This mysterious gentleman is a master of the subtleties of the game. We'd better stop fraternizing before he seduces us into contemplation of its mysteries and we forget we have a match to play."

"Forgive me, sir," Vance said softly, "I've spoken too much already." Again he withdrew, a subtle touch to Junah steering him toward his own practice lane.

Keeler's eyes followed as they withdrew. "Sir, tell me," he called after Junah, "was your caddie ever a professional somewhere?"

Junah laughed. "He's been that and a lot more."

Keeler absorbed this thoughtfully. "May I ask where, sir?" he called, this time directly to Bagger Vance. "Where were you a professional?"

Photographers and spectators had overheard the exchange. There was a stir; a dozen pairs of eyes, including Junah's, turned to Bagger Vance to see if he would answer. The caddie squinted back toward Keeler. His voice was low, barely audible. "Here," he said. "I was a professional here."

Keeler blinked, uncertain how to take this. Was the fellow mocking him? Keeler's eyes searched Vance's for a flicker of jest or ridicule. Jones too paused in his routine. You could see them both, confronted by the mystery of Vance's clear truthful gaze, pull themselves, even shake themselves back to their centers. *Let this be*—their postures straightened and refocused—*we have a match to play.* At that moment, a commotion rippled from the rear of the gallery. We heard an automobile horn honk. Into view at the end of the tee eased Hagen's brand-new Auburn six-door.

The car stopped and the chauffeur sprung out. He clapped his own door shut, then stepped swiftly around to the rear. You could glimpse a head of blond curls behind the smoked glass and hear girlish laughter pealing. The chauffeur tugged the rear door open. There was a pregnant beat, a wafting curl of tobacco smoke, then a $500 black-and-white golf shoe arced forth into the sunlight, followed by an athletic calf wrapped in pale yellow argyle and a knife-creased plus four. Sir Walter stepped forth in his plumage. A breath expelled from the gallery, and then applause sprung, reinforced by cheers and shouts of excitement.

Hagen's caddie, Spec Hammond, stepped first onto the tee. Then his footman, in equestrian boots to the knee; then a boy, like me, bearing refreshments, including cigarettes in a silver case (I heard someone behind me say Hagen always had quail eggs carried with him on-course, as a snack and to keep up his strength). Then the Haig himself strode forth.

Jones had turned back and was witnessing this with a wry smile, having no doubt endured this assault of style and gamesmanship many times in the past. The gallery too recognized this psychological salvo; it was a joke they were in on and they loved it.

"You boys get enough breakfast in you?" Hagen called gaily to Jones and Junah. "I've got hot coffee in the Auburn if you want." He thumped his stomach contentedly and gave a belch of satisfaction. The gallery laughed and turned to each other in merry whispers.

"A nice jolt of caffeine, that's just what our nerves need," Keeler grinned back to appreciative laughter from the gallery. Photographers and reporters were clustering around Hagen now; Jones returned to his warm-up, moving from short irons to mid-irons; then Junah started, I scampered out onto the range with the shag bag as he lobbed the first easy pitches. It was a grand perspective. I was out there, fifty or sixty yards, on the immaculately manicured grass. I could see the gallery, in colorful thousands now and swelling each moment, with the hotel rising behind and the Atlantic pounding in mightily beyond the dunes.

My position was on the right. Jones' shag boy stood in the middle, a hundred yards behind, and Hagen's was now trotting out, deep, going way back toward the fence. I could hear Jones' mid-irons hissing overhead, hear the backspin loud and sizzling; the balls dropped so close to the shag boy he could collect them with just a step this way or that. On the left of the tee, Hagen was finishing with the reporters. He didn't tee his own ball, but had Spec do it. His shag boy was most of the way back at the fence, 250 yards out. Hagen took his driver, gave it a swift waggle and stepped right to the ball. This was odd; players normally warm up through the short irons, mids and longs, taking out the distance clubs only at the very end when they're thoroughly warmed up. But here the Haig was brandishing his driver right out of the slot. The gallery hushed. Every eye, including Jones' and Junah's fans', turned as Hagen planted his feet, waggled once, cocked an eye down the range and lashed at the ball with all his strength.

He cold-topped it! The ball squirted dead into the turf and rebounded with a flat, sickening sound, to bound and shoot away, a sharp 180-yard grounder. The gallery gasped with shock, then laughed with release of tension as it saw the twinkle in the Haig's eye. "Sorry, Bob," Hagen grinned across at the center slot, where Jones endured this patiently.

Spec teed another ball; the Haig slashed; a duck hook shot

dead left off his clubhead, overspinning wildly and nose-diving into the dirt 40 yards out, bounding away into the weeds. The gallery was now thoroughly enjoying itself, snorting and rollicking, each spectator no doubt rehearsing the story as he or she would tell it tonight and for decades into the future.

I had to keep my eye on Junah, who was trying to maintain focus on his own practice. He had hit half a dozen nice smooth lofters, all right at my feet (one had bounced clean into the shag bag). But now I saw something that froze my blood. That same grim, distanced look on Junah's face. That posture of despair. The more the gallery enjoyed Hagen's high jinks, the darker the cloud grew over Junah's head. What was he thinking? What was tormenting him?

Hagen's caddie teed a third ball; this the Haig blasted in exactly the opposite direction, a wild towering slice that arced across the 150-yard-wide practice area and vanished into the cattails on the far right. I saw Keeler take out a bill from his wallet and lay it wordlessly on the ground beside the slot where Jones was rifling his mid-irons; Jones produced a bill of his own and set it beside Keeler's. Spec bent to tee Sir Walter's fourth ball. Dramatically Hagen stopped him several inches short of the turf. The Haig teed it himself, then doffed his cream-colored jacket and stepped to the ball, loose and easy in just his shirt and tie.

He swung. The ball rocketed off the clubface, nailed cold solid, and boomed downrange in an ever-climbing trajectory, finally steaming to earth well past the shag boy, sending the fellow scampering back to the 275 mark to overtake the still-galloping ball. The gallery roared. I saw Keeler bend to the ground, pick up both bills and hand them to Jones, who with a wry grin slipped them into his pocket.

Then I looked back at Junah. Jones had his spoon out now and was banging his first balls for distance. The crowd oohed and ahhed as the great champion's shots thundered down the range. Hagen, at his end of the tee, was cracking jokes. The gallery was laughing. Junah's shoulders seemed to slump even more. His shots were getting ragged. Jones had gone to his driver now; he began launching bombs into the fence, then halfway up, then clean over. A pack of boys outside scuffled madly over each ball, the victor thrusting his trophy aloft, then surging afresh with the mob as the next ball, Hagen's now, came sailing clear and bounding beside them.

Junah had stopped hitting. He was at mid-iron range. I had moved back, just shy of the 175; Hagen's shag boy was past the 275, Jones' all the way to the fence. I could hear the Chief Marshal shout, "Twenty minutes to tee time!" Junah put his mid-iron away and took no other. What was he doing? Going to the putting green? Without hitting any long irons or woods? I felt the skin on my back go cold with gooseflesh.

Junah was saying something to Bagger Vance, something cross and impatient. Oh no. I could see him peer out toward the ocean, to the sand mounds that ran the length of the first fairway. The dune line for a quarter mile was packed with spectators, thousands and thousands, already massing three and four deep like some vast army drawing up in line of battle. Junah turned with that despairing look I had come so to dread. *Hit a ball*, the voice in my head was shouting to him. Then to Vance: *Set a ball out, stick a club in his hand!* I could see Vance do just that. But Junah wouldn't take it. His eyes swung south to the entry drive, the six-mile approach to the hotel where fresh multitudes now advanced from parking areas. I saw Jones glance over, just for a moment, toward Junah. He too sensed something awry. I wanted to rush in, though God only knows what I hoped to accomplish, but I didn't dare. I held my position 175 yards out, feeling like a fool as the other shag boys chased down their men's balls and I could do nothing but stand there useless and waiting.

Then Junah moved. Slowly at first, then with increasing resolve, off the tee, into the gallery which parted without resistance, no doubt assuming the competitor was on his way to the practice green to warm up his putter. I seized the shag bag and tore in on a dead run. Junah was through the crowd now, approaching the Chalmers. This was the signal of alarm. No need of a car to cross forty yards to the putting green. Judge Anderson came striding, there was no mistaking his face flushed with anger; my father hurried forward too. Junah brushed past them both, and several other elders, calling behind him to Bagger Vance, ordering the caddie to come along, hurry.

Vance obeyed, striding in Junah's wake with the bag and clubs. The elders pursued, demanding to know Junah's intentions. I raced up just as this urgent knot reached the Chalmers.

"Throw my clubs in back," Junah commanded Bagger Vance. "Take me away from here!"

"To where, sir?"

"Out there, away from this crush, where I can think!"

He pointed to the open duneland between the two massed armies, then plunged into the darkness of the backseat and slammed the door. Bagger Vance set the bag swiftly into the trunk and sprang obediently behind the wheel. The engine snarled to life. Judge Anderson was rapping indignantly on Junah's smoked window, demanding to know where his champion was going. Junah called the more fiercely to Vance, "Get me out of here!"

The Chalmers lurched. The crowd parted before it. Judge Anderson, his fury constrained only by the necessity at all costs of avoiding a scene, hissed for marshals, officers, anyone to stop the vehicle. It was too late, the auto was gathering pace. I leapt onto the running board opposite the chauffeur's window, clutching the tea jug and rucksack as the car bucked away toward the dunes.

"Stay with him, Hardy," I could hear the Judge shout. "Tell us what the hell is going on!"

Thirteen

THE CHALMERS PULLED UP ON A SAND RIDGE beyond the greenskeeper's road that paralleled the eighth and ninth fairways. You could see the galleries surging along the high ground adjacent to the first and second, seeking position for the match's start. Number one was already encircled tee to green in ranks three and four deep; thousands and thousands of white shirts and neckties, crew hats and panamas and boaters, ladies' parasols and periscopes, the first shock troops rolling into position across the turf's undulations, while their later fellows swept along the flanks in skirmish lines, rushing ahead to form their perimeters along fairway number two. All these the Chalmers bypassed, seeking the high ground beyond. The car stopped and the parking brake cranked on; before Bagger Vance stepped out I had already sprung from the running board and scampered to the rear, hauled Junah's golf bag from the trunk, not even sure why except perhaps hoping to inspire the champion with the sight of his weapons, and whisked it around to the auto's flank. The ridge itself was a brilliant vantage, elevated, sealed off from the multitudes by several hundred yards of duneland, with an unbroken vista out over the sand plain to the ocean. To the west the view was clear back to the hotel's spires, the bright canvas of its tourney tents and the fresh thousands swarming in from the entry drives and the auto lots. From the Chalmers' rear door Junah now emerged. He didn't step fully forth, but came half forward, shoulders and torso into the doorframe, placed one spiked sole before him into the sand, then sat slowly onto the running board and lowered his head into his hands.

"Put the clubs away, Hardy," he said in a voice nearly inaudible. "I see no profit in them or this whole fool enterprise."

I turned desperately to Bagger Vance. The caddie as always was the soul of composure. He motioned me to set the bag down, there in the dune grass beside the champion.

"Your mind is clearly in torment, Junah," Bagger Vance spoke slowly and evenly. "Tell me please: what is the nature of your complaint?"

Junah glanced up sharply at this word, which seemed to trivialize his emotion. "It couldn't be more obvious, could it?" He gestured toward the multitudes in their bright battle lines, visible across the linksland. "This whole endeavor is a freak show. A joke. What good will any of it do me, or anyone attached to it?"

"I perceive much good," Bagger Vance replied in that same even tone. "But tell me more specifically, what is it *you* perceive?"

Junah's eyes remained cast down. You could see his shoulders tremble and broaden as anger, long and deeply held, began to swell powerfully within him.

" 'Victory' and 'defeat' "—he spat the words with revulsion, as if their very sound were obscene—"I'm sick to death of them, and of men contending as if there was any difference between them! What good ever came of human beings facing one another in conflict? To see men of such stature as Jones and Hagen steeling themselves for this child's game, it was all I could do to keep from howling with hysteria, or despair, which would have been more appropriate. While the world is coming apart, our countrymen starving by the millions . . . here we disport ourselves, chasing a dimpled ball across a millionaire's playground. And for what? An heiress' greed and desperation? A few dollars to be scraped from our visitors' pockets, the pathetic need of Savannah's war-haunted psyche to 'redeem itself'—and through my efforts! I won't do it. I won't be a part of this circus.

"They're here for blood," he said, gesturing with contempt toward the distant hosts, "make no mistake about it. To see men contend against each other, hoping to watch one or all be torn and fall. This is war, for all its summer cottons and ladies' frocks, and nothing good ever came from that." Junah's hands were trembling. He ran them in pain through his hair, eyes gazing hollowly before him into the dunes. "What is ever gained by 'defeating' others? What can be gained here today? If I win I take no pleasure, and if I lose . . ."

Here Junah's voice choked and broke off; not, one felt, with the thought of his own possible defeat or disgrace, but with the overweening futility of contention itself, which even at my tender age I could see he had wrestled with long and hard.

Junah's eyes rose now and met Bagger Vance's. "I have been a warrior," he said in a voice tremulous with emotion. "I have fought, and nearly died, in battles as grave and calamitous as any in the history of man. I have seen friends perish, and enemies who might have been friends but for the madness of war. I will never take up arms again"—he gestured toward the bag and its clubs—"even surrogates as preposterous as these."

Saying this, Junah slumped yet deeper onto the running board, his mind tormented by grief.

Now Bagger Vance spoke. "This conduct is disgraceful," he said. "Unworthy of any man, but more so of you, Rannulph Junah, whom I hold dear and bless beyond all others. Get ahold of yourself! It provokes me to fury, to see you cast down your eyes and give voice to such ignoble thoughts!"

Vance's tone had changed utterly. He did not, and never did in my hearing, regress to rage; rather he spoke with a fiery primordial force and emphasis. Junah's eyes rose again, shaken by the tone of his servant's voice.

"What do you know of life?" Bagger Vance stood before the champion. "Are you a god that you have plumbed the depths of existence's meaning? What statement can you make about what is real or important? Have you pierced the veil? When you have, then you may display the temerity to which you now presume! Despair. Death. You know nothing of them! Are you a god? Then shut up and do your duty!"

Junah started to speak, but Bagger Vance's force overrode him. "What if I tell you that before a thimbleful of sand has slipped through the glass, one of your opponents today will need another man's hand simply to rise from his chair . . . and the other will have passed into eternity? What if I tell you of your own death? And how swiftly it follows on the heels of this disgraceful moment?

"And war, since you yourself raise the subject. Shall I tell you of another conflagration coming—soon, Junah, soon—which will dwarf your Great War, breaking nations and peoples in their millions and culminating in horrors beyond the race's imagining?"

Junah's countenance was now chastened, even fearstruck. He looked up at his servant, with pure heartbreak in his eyes. "You upbraid me as if I were a child, and no doubt I deserve it. But please don't abandon me. Do you think I want to feel these awful emotions, that I take pleasure in the desperate conclusions my heart leads me to? I'm lost, Bagger. Help me, my friend and mentor. Tell me what I must do."

Across the dunes now sped a Krewe Island station car, a marshal's vehicle, with a blue-blazered official driving and Dougal McDermott white-faced in the passenger seat. Its high undercarriage skimmed clear, approaching fast over the tufted greenskeeper's road.

It was coming for us. Beyond, we could see the galleries massed in readiness, swollen to six and seven deep along the first fairway. Jones and Hagen had finished on the practice green. You could see their party, moving along the crested path to the first tee.

"We have spoken in jest many times, you and I," Bagger Vance addressed Junah, "about why I initially attached myself to you, and why I've never strayed far from your side all these years. It was for this day, Junah. As we go, I will teach you."

He nodded to me; I bent to the golf bag and passed it to him. Bagger Vance set it upright before the champion, its hickory-shafted irons flashing like quivered arrows in the sun. The Krewe Island car pulled up alongside us. Across the duneland you could hear the galleries cheer as Hagen and Jones approached the first tee.

"Your heart is kind, Junah. You have seen the agony of war and you wish never again to harm anything or anyone. So you choose not to act. As if by that choice, you will cause no harm.

"This intention is admirable as far as it goes, but it fails to apprehend the deeper imperative of life. Life *is* action, Junah. Even choosing not to act, we act. We cannot do otherwise. Therefore act with vigor!"

Vance glanced once to McDermott, to let the professional know we were coming. Then he turned back to his champion.

"Stand now, Junah, and take your place. Do honor to yourself and to your station!"

Fourteen

MORE THAN SIXTY YEARS HAVE PASSED since that day, yet I can still bring to mind as vividly as if I were witnessing them this instant every shot as it flew and every putt as it rolled. Most excruciating were the first six holes, which I cannot recall even at this remove without wincing. But here, Michael. Let the card speak with its own eloquence.

This is not Junah's actual card, the one Jones kept, with his and Junah's signatures. That relic vanished mysteriously after the match and was never recovered, despite the fevered efforts of Savannah's sporting scribes, the Chamber of Commerce, several University of Georgia historians and the local chapter of the Daughters of the Confederacy. No, this is the card I kept as a double-check, following Bagger Vance's instructions and under pain, I felt, of eternal damnation should I slip and record a hole incorrectly. Here, against a par of 5 4 4 3, is Junah's tally for the first four holes:

6   5   4   5

The first he bogeyed ignominiously by dumping a pitch of twenty yards smack into a bunker and barely struggling out onto the fringe. He followed this with an equally egregious bogey on number two, duck-hooking his drive so viciously that it wound up in rough behind the gallery and found a playable lie only by the chance of coming to rest in a trampled area near some portable toilets. The third Junah parred without incident, allowing the Savannah gallery its first normal breath in half an hour. But then he sent them into paroxyms on the par-three fourth, double-bogeying it like the sorriest hacker with a half-shanked mid-iron and a three-putt from eleven feet.

Hagen's card, with two birdies and a bogey, read:

4   4   3   4

And Jones':

5   4   4   3

In other words, Junah had fallen five medal strokes behind in the first four holes!

His card would have been even more appalling over the next two except for a stroke of blind luck at the fifth, an eminently birdieable par four of 378 yards that Junah was butchering mightily, lying two in a bunker 30 yards short of the green. From here, out of a clean playable lie, he cold-skulled a sand iron, sending the ball rocketing across the green, the far-side gallery ducking in terror as it screamed toward them at an altitude of five feet, when it struck the pin and dropped straight into the hole. A birdie! Junah bogeyed the sixth after letting a driving iron get away from him in the wind, watching it dive-bomb into the left wall of a revetted greenside bunker and having to pitch rearward just to get a chip at the green. Still he hadn't lost any more strokes on those two, as Hagen and Jones parred both.

We now stood on the seventh tee. The state of the Savannah gallery was approaching apoplexy. Judge Neskaloosa River Anderson looked ready to burst from the crush and strangle Junah personally, while it was all my father could do to force his eyes to watch. Junah's swing, which for grace and power was every inch the equal of Jones', was utterly gone. He couldn't even take his grip. You could see his hands struggling futilely to find position on the leather. Nothing fit. His fingers looked bloated and swollen. The club was an alien instrument; he couldn't set his hands on it right no matter how he tried.

But let me recount the gallery's emotions from my father's recollections, which I heard him tell and retell in subsequent years at various cocktail parties and club dances. This, the tale from his point of view as he strode the galleries with Judge Anderson, Joel Dees and Dr. Eben Syracuse, the three most prominent elders.

As Junah's play got worse [my father invariably began the tale], I feared not just for his reputation but for his life. These birds wanted his scalp. None more so than Judge Anderson, who had been his most ardent champion what seemed like mere moments ago. How they hated him now! "What the hell's wrong with his grip?" Anderson clutched my arm as tight as a tourniquet. "He looks like he's holding his pecker out there, not a goddamn golf club!"

Junah was not trying hard enough. He was trying too hard. He didn't give a damn about Savannah. He cared so much he was freezing up. "By God, look at his Adam's apple," Judge Anderson declared in a voice raging with frustration. "If he was choking any harder, he'd suffocate on the spot!"

The solons began casting about for ways to pull Junah off the course. A fabricated emergency. An injury. Anything to bring this ignominious display to a swift and merciful close. "If I ever open my fool mouth again," the Judge declared of his idea that recruited Junah in the first place, "shoot me and put me out of my misery!"

It was inevitable that the elders' wrath would swing from Junah, who despite their frustration in this painful moment they nonetheless acknowledged to be a patrician and a hero, to some more easily sacrificeable target. His caddie. The mysterious stranger, Bagger Vance. "What the hell advice is that sonofabitch giving him?" Dr. Syracuse fumed as Junah took his excruciating rearward stance in the bunker on the sixth. "He hasn't stopped talking since the first tee! Look at him, he's lecturing the man! Insolent bastard. Since when did he become Harry Goddamn Vardon?" The Judge and Syracuse ordered Dees to get closer, to find out what fool nonsense the caddie was stuffing into their champion's ear.

Crossing from the green Dees succeeded. He scurried back to us with his report. "He's talking about detachment. Telling Junah not to root for his ball. Don't say, 'Get legs!' or 'Bite!' Just let it be." "Don't root for his ball? What the hell does *that* mean?" Judge Anderson thundered. Dees continued, "He's telling Junah to release the shot mentally the instant he hits it, not to be attached to where it lands or what happens to it."

The Judge declared that the most damn-fool thing he had ever heard. How the hell can you play golf and not care where the ball goes? He caught up with the caddie on the rise just below the tee and demanded an explanation. Vance coolly explained that he would be glad to address the subject in detail at a later date but that now he must focus all his energy on assisting Junah. "You've done a helluva job of assisting him so far," the Judge snorted in fury. The caddie's unruffled calm enraged the elders. This was no time for philosophy. Junah's swing was gone. His plane was out, his rhythm was shot, his timing was nonexistent! What was wrong with him? What on God's earth was his problem and what on God's earth could we do about it?

Here the caddie, who had been moving with the players'

and gallery's flow toward the tee, stopped, turned and met the elders' eyes.

"Junah's problem is simple," he said. "He thinks he is Junah."

"What in damnation does that mean?" The Judge's face flushed crimson. "He *is* Junah, you damn twit!"

"I will teach him he is not Junah," the caddie answered with his accustomed calm. "Then he will swing Junah's swing."

Vance turned and climbed powerfully up the slope to the seventh tee. Anderson wheeled to Dees, Syracuse and me. "I don't care what the Rules say"—the Judge jerked his thumb in Bagger Vance's direction—"get that lunatic sonofabitch off Junah's bag!"

Of course the Judge couldn't. The Rules of Golf forbade replacement of a caddie other than in an emergency or for voluntary withdrawal, and Bagger Vance was not about to withdraw, voluntarily or otherwise.

In fact on that tee he came forward and more powerfully than ever seized control of Junah, to my own shock and even horror, and to that portion of the gallery who overheard the exchange.

"Why don't you hook this one out of bounds?" Bagger Vance spoke directly to the champion, wiping a new Spalding, a high-compression black Dot, as he readied to hand it to him. I was there, not three feet away, and couldn't believe my ears. Neither could Junah. For an instant he tried to take it as a joke. Surely Bagger Vance was trying to loosen his man up with a little reverse psychology. One look in the caddie's eyes dispelled that no-tion. Vance placed the ball in Junah's hand and tugged the over-size persimmon driver up from the bag. "Just snipe it over that first bunker, it'll hit the road and bound off to hell and gone. Then you'll be so far out of the match, you can relax."

Junah stared at him stricken. Golfers in general are suggest-ible, and never more so than under the pressure of a desperate match. Junah knew (as did I, and the closely pressed part of the gallery including Judge Anderson, Dees, Syracuse and my fa-ther, who overheard) that merely to give voice to such a prospect was to guarantee its happening. Junah would step to the tee with that horrifying self-fulfilling thought in mind and . . . "Go on"—Bagger Vance pressed Schenectady Slim, the driver, into the champion's hand—"what are you waiting for?"

Hagen and Jones had already driven; Jones about 260 down the right side, Hagen five or ten yards to Jones' rear, in the cen-ter. Now Junah stepped between the markers. His hands were trembling as he set his right leg back and bent over his left, using the driver for balance as he stretched down to tee the ball; you could see the dimples and the little arched Spalding logo wobble atop their wooden perch. Junah actually had to steady the ball with three fingers to keep it from tumbling. He rose, shaken, and tried to settle, shifting and rocking and replanting his spiked soles into a comfortable address position. There. He had his stance. He waggled. A swift glance to Bagger Vance, as if plead-ing for a reprieve. But the caddie's eyes met Junah's sternly; Vance even threw a curt nod for emphasis, as if to say, What's keeping you, get to it!

Junah swung. You could hear the sickening turnover blow as the ball arced hard off the clubface, left and low, then dove even farther left, spinning furiously over the exact bunker Bagger Vance had indicated, striking the greenskeeper's road precisely as he had said, and bounding wildly to vanish into the marsh grass. Out of bounds. Stroke and distance. Tee another one.

The gallery groaned. Junah couldn't bear to look up. He certainly couldn't make his eyes meet Bagger Vance's. I saw Jones and Hagen exchange a glance of pity, then avert their gazes simultaneously, eyes lowering to an absent focus on the turf. The match, or Junah's inclusion in it, had reached its nadir. It had become an embarrassment, a joke, a fiasco. It hurt Jones and Hagen. Cheapened them. And everyone knew it would only get worse. No one rallies from the place Junah inhabited now. Jones knew it, Hagen knew it, the gallery knew it and most painful of all Junah knew it. A stony misery settled over his handsome features. He stepped with numb resignation, like a captive condemned not just to execution but to a lingering public humiliation beforehand, back toward his caddie, who now paused before placing a second ball in the champion's palm.

"Do you want to quit?" Vance spoke quietly, so Junah and I alone could hear. "We can easily fabricate an excuse that will be embraced by everyone. No disgrace. No one will quibble with your parting under these circumstances, least of all your friends." Vance indicated the Judge and the other elders who hovered painfully in a knot at the rear of the tee. "They will be grateful to you."

Junah used his thumbnail to scrape a small clod of soil from the soleplate of his driver. "You know I can't quit," he answered.

Vance nodded gravely, then dropped the fresh ball into Junah's palm. "I know it," he said. "I wanted to make sure you did."

Fifteen

A N ATHLETE OF YOUR CALIBER, Michael, can well imagine Junah's state of mind at this juncture. But to bring it
into even bolder relief, let me show you something.

It's a magazine article by Arnold Langer. Remember, the
writer from the *Atlanta Constitution* who mesmerized my mother
and father over breakfast with tales of Junah's heroism in the
War. The article did not appear until two years after the match
in the Summer of '33 issue of *Susquehanna Quarterly*. This may
seem an odd place for a piece of sports journalism except that
Langer, as you will see, sensed that an event of significance beyond sport was taking place and therefore submitted his piece to
a more serious journal. If you skim the first pages, you'll see the
article covers a number of sports: it refers to Dempsey, Tilden,
Lou Gehrig; quite a bit of it is about prize fighting. It's not until
page 4 that Langer, advancing his line of thought, turns to the
match at Krewe Island.

GRACE UNDER FIRE

The writer covering a variety of athletic endeavors is inevitably asked by acquaintances to render an assessment as to which sport is the most difficult, which tests the competitor to the utmost. Most expect the response to be a physically violent sport, perhaps football or ski racing, or one in which danger to life and limb predominates, as in motor racing or alpine mountaineering.

These acquaintances are invariably startled (and occasionally outraged) when I without hesitation declare that Supreme Sport to be golf.

Golf is the most grueling sport, the most testing sport, the sport which more than any other strips the competitor bare, mentally, psychologically and emotionally. Rarely have I seen this demonstrated more vividly and painfully than in the 1931 exhibition match at Krewe Island, Georgia. Here before our horrified eyes, the sporting press witnessed a man of unassailable credentials in courage, Captain Rannulph Junah, a decorated officer and bona fide war hero, come utterly undone under the pressure of what one would think would be to a man of his grim experience the merest trifle. A golf match.

One watched the opening nine holes of that contest with an emotion that can only be described as horror. Your heart broke for the Captain, who was so clearly overmatched, not so much in a technical sense (his shotmaking capabilities were very nearly the equal of Jones' and Hagen's) as the psychological. That aspect of mind, that discipline which enables one to retain his focus on that peculiarly mental battlefield we know as golf.

Consider Jones for a moment. Bobby's swing, for all the adulatory prose it has inspired over the years, possesses a number of flaws, which Jones himself would be the first to acknowledge. His footwork has always been suspect, he invariably overrotates his hips when straining for distance and, most heretical of all, his grip at the top of the backswing quite frequently comes loose! His fingers partially release the club, then regrip as he starts down. But these flaws, which in a lesser mortal would spell calamity, are overridden by Jones' spectacular cardinal virtue: his rhythm.

Jones has been quoted on the subject, to which he confesses in his typical self-deprecatory fashion that he has devoted far too many hours of study. "Rhythm and confidence are twin names for the same quicksilver element. They are two sides of the same coin; rhythm the physical manifestation, confidence the mental. You may start with either; it will irresistibly produce the other."

In other words for Jones, rhythm is the touchstone, the haven, the physical/mental core around which he centers himself and from which he draws his confidence.

Hagen on the other hand can never be accused of anything so civilized as rhythm. The Haig's wild lurching motion is almost laughable alongside Jones' languid Olympian tempo. Everything is hands, arms and the slashing wristwork for Sir Walter. Yet Hagen, like Jones, possesses an equally unbreachable harbor: his profound and uncanny feel for the clubhead. That gift of consciousness, that absolute sense of where the blade is, its precise orbit and alignment at all times in the swing's wheeling constellation.

What makes Hagen so exciting to watch is his capacity for midcourse corrections. He will seem to topple, roll, lurch, yet so sure is his sense of the clubhead that even from some wildly off-balance posture he manages somehow to right himself and recover in midswing, whipping the blade back to true and slashing the shot home. Then of course he'll wink as if he had that very stroke in mind all along.

Hagen does it with clubhead sense, Jones with tempo. But both do it with the mind. That is what makes them champions.

Now consider our struggling warrior, Captain Junah. Junah's swing, unlike Jones' and Hagen's was merely perfect. He stood to the ball flawlessly, his backswing unfolded straight from the copybook, his move through the ball was poetry itself. Yet all this availed him nothing under the pressure of the match. Over the ball the hero seemed to fall not so much into a state of fear as a fog of confusion. Of disfocus. He was lost. He looked, I don't know what other word to use, innocent. I recall his caddie, a peculiarly intense fellow, struggling mightily to steady him. The bag carrier kept up a nearly constant monologue, apparently of counsel and instruction which, on this front nine at least, seemed more to un-nerve the competitor than to rally him.

So is it courage then? Is it physical courage, the kind required in wartime, that equates to success on the field of golfing combat? Apparently not. Apparently some other quality is needed. A quality which Jones and Hagen possessed but which Captain Junah, at least over the first nine holes, did not.

It is my thesis that performance under fire (in the lesser world of sport, at least) is not a function of physical courage, but of consciousness. Of awareness.

Or, perhaps more accurately, awakeness.

This is not conscious awakeness, I believe. It doesn't spring from the front of the brain. Its source is rather, I suspect, something far deeper, proceeding from a far more profound quadrant of consciousness.

Jones and Hagen, in this match as in their other championships, were both capable of rising to necessity. Not, I believe, because of any superiority in their physical swings. But because of their ability to center themselves in a quality of consciousness which linked them absolutely and vividly to what they were doing. Jones with his rhythm and Hagen with his feel for the clubhead were capable of remaining connected to the moment via some mysterious current of consciousness, an awakeness, an immersion that rendered them capable of correcting and adjusting in midswing, enabling them under pressure to deliver shots which lesser mortals are incapable of. Let me draw it to a finer point. Their swings are capable of responding to their wills.

What is the nature of this will, this awakeness? Where does it reside? And how can we tap into it?

We could ask Jones, but for all his brilliance, he has never been able to articulate it. Sir Walter is wise enough not to try. Perhaps we should ask Captain Junah, who wrestled with it so valiantly.

Or maybe we should ask his caddie.

Langer was being facetious, of course, and even condescending. What he didn't know was that he was dead right.

I stuck tight beside Bagger Vance through seven, eight, and nine and he kept pounding Junah relentlessly, demanding an answer to the same question:

"Who are you, Junah?"

Vance would ask this, then answer for Junah, keeping up an unbroken harangue as they strode from shot to shot.

"Tell me who you are, Junah. Who, in your deepest parts, when all that is inauthentic has been stripped away. Are you your name, Rannulph Junah? Will that hit this shot for you? Are you your illustrious forebears? Will they hit it?

"Are you your roles, Junah? Scion, soldier, Southerner? Husband, father, lover? Slayer of the foe in battle, comforter of the friend at home? Are you your virtues, Junah, or your sins? Your deeds, your feats? Are you your dreams or your nightmares? Tell me, Junah. Can you hit the ball with any of these?"

Junah tried to stammer no. . . .

"No?" Vance pressed yet harder, "Then who *are* you? Answer me!"

We were crossing between the nines now. The surge to the tenth tee carried the massed throngs away from the ocean to a run of five inland holes. The gallery's weight and depth seemed to cut off all breeze; the heat hit you like a blast oven. The backs of Jones' and Hagen's shirts were drenched with sweat as we climbed the rise to the tenth tee. Junah removed his hat and buried his face in a towel; the moisture was dripping from it; I gave him tea and an apple and a big chunk of ice, which he wrapped in his pocket kerchief and applied to his burning neck.

The big scoreboard by the tourney tents was visible when he reached the height of the tee. Hagen 35, Jones 36, Junah 41. The nine behind felt like a war zone; it seemed impossible that the competitors still had a siege of 27 more holes to play.

I watched Junah peer around, trying to gather himself. The massed humanity, the heat, the blistering sun; across the dunes the galleries surged in massed battalions, one hole ahead, two holes ahead, swarming over brows of ridges in a relentless advance, flanking and maneuvering for position. Junah's face was flushed; you could see his temples pound. He was not here on Krewe Island, but somewhere else, somewhere . . .

"Yes, this is war, Junah. As you said before."

Bagger Vance moved beside the champion on the tee. "But this war is not between you and your opponents, or even you and the course. No, Junah, this battle like Reality itself takes place on a higher plane. The plane of the Self.

"That higher battle is the one you are losing, Junah. It is why you are losing here."

Jones lashed a monster down the right side, a screaming yardage-devouring hook that arced out and back over the rough, hit the fairway steaming and bounded forward with overspin to slow finally, curling safely around the flank of a bunker I'd paced off the night before at 285.

Junah barely noticed, so tightly was he held by Bagger Vance's eyes. "What can I do, Bagger? Tell me."

Hagen was stepping to tee his ball; Vance kept his voice low. "I require only one thing of you, Junah. That you swing your True Swing. Your Authentic Swing."

"What the hell do you think I want?" Junah hissed. "How do I do it?"

He paused for Hagen's address. Sir Walter ripped one, a high dead-straight boomer that was all carry, splitting the middle and landing just a few yards behind Jones', settling onto a clean flat lie, 190 from the 464-yard green. The applause echoed; then the gallery turned to Junah, who still stood over his bag, his face inches from his caddie's.

"Who are you, Junah? Nothing you call yourself can help you now. I have emptied you of all that. This match, this heat, this day have emptied you.

"Listen to me." Vance moved closer yet as the gallery shifted impatiently, wondering what the hell was keeping Junah from the tee. "All your 'selves' are exhausted and gone. Now: hit the ball with what is left."

Junah's glance was desperate. "But there's *nothing* left."

Vance nodded. "Exactly."

The caddie held out the champion's driver.

"Remember, the game is simple. The ball doesn't move. It simply sits and waits. Now strike it, Junah. Hold nothing back. Hit it with everything you have."

Vance set Schenectady Slim in Junah's hands. You could see the champion's head was whirling, his brain beyond overload. The gallery sensed an apocalypse. Hagen and Jones did too. I was in terror that Junah might faint, collapse, actually fall down, so dizzy and disoriented did he seem. I shut my eyes, too terrified to watch as Junah teed his ball and stepped to it. I squinted to see him look back at Vance, one last time. Then he set himself, glanced once down the fairway . . .

Junah's clubhead started back. Before it reached the top, the gallery knew. Judge Anderson knew, my father knew, everyone who had ever seen and marveled at Junah's swing when it was on

. . . they all knew. He was on plane. On track. On rails. The big persimmon hit the slot at the top exactly, you could see Junah's wrists cock fully into their ultimate power position, his knees and hips had already started rotating forward into the shot as the clubhead reached its zenith, high and geometric, left arm at full extension, and then, not with a slash or a blast but almost in slow motion the club powered through the hitting zone. The sound was like a bomb. The gallery gasped as the ball exploded off the clubface, low and hissing fire, and boomed down the narrow alley between the massed formations. Heads snapped, trying to follow its speed. There was a quick intake of breath, then a joyous release of tension, applause and a rush of awe and appreciation. I looked at Jones and saw a small curl of pleasure in his lip; he appreciated it too. Hagen was already striding off the tee, head down, ignoring the shot, which meant of course he had seen it and took it seriously. I peered toward the far right bunker, the one Jones' ball had rolled to, whose carry paced off at 285. Junah's drive cleared it on the fly, took one long hard hop, then settled into a low, ground-hugging roll, coming to rest 30 yards farther on, 315 from the tee, with Tawdry Jones the forecaddie sprinting in its wake to jubilantly plant his bright white flag. Three-fifteen cold. Thirty yards past Jones, nearly 40 beyond Hagen.

Junah himself could barely believe it. Not so much the prodigiousness of the blow, as he had hit many as well and better, but that somehow it had appeared at this time, when his swing had seemed utterly incapable of producing it. He turned to Bagger Vance, as if expecting a winking smile or a thumbs-up. But the caddie was already striding for the fairway, instructing me to give Junah another of my iced apples and make sure he ate it. "You *are* your swing, Junah," he muttered to the champion as he passed. "We will find that swing today and, having found it, nothing will ever take it from you again."

Sixteen

J UNAH BIRDIED TEN, eleven and twelve. I can't overstate the emotional effect that had upon the gallery, and not just the Savannah contingent. The sweltering thousands had shared Junah's agony through the front nine . . . as golfers they understood his torment. Now the pendulum swung mercifully back; the gallery responded with a rush of glorious relief. None believed Junah's spree would last. That he would fall apart again was inevitable, given how shaky he was. But at least, thank God, he had been granted these three holes. These would comfort him in memory. These we others could brag about, these we could tell and retell.

Junah's pitch finished eight feet below the pin on ten; he rammed the putt dead down the throat. This sounds better than it was. In fact Junah's stone-numb hands banged the putt like a jackhammer; had the ball not collided dead-on with the back of the cup, it would have shot four or five feet past. You could see

Junah clinging to what slight composure he had regained, desperate for some clear concrete focus to hold him together. I kept tight beside Vance as he strode at Junah's elbow toward eleven. This was the first time I heard the caddie speak on the subject of the grip.

"You're in your head, Junah, I need you to come down into your hands. Listen to me. Intelligence, I have told you, does not reside in the brain but in the hands. Let them do the thinking, they're far wiser than you are. Be patient. Let the club settle. Don't make a move toward the ball until the leather has found its proper nestle. Remember, the hands do not create the swing, they *find* it, they *remember* it. Do you recall in the East how the *sadhus* would sit, palms upturned in contemplation, making antennas of their hands? The golfer's hands are his antennas too, searching the Field, drawing in the Authentic Swing."

"What 'Field'?" Junah interrupted impatiently. "I'm sorry, Bagger, I can't absorb all this." Vance nodded with patience, touching Junah gently on the elbow, steering him onto the next tee. Eleven was a short but severe dogleg left, across bunkers to a deceptively shallow fairway that could be easily overdriven into unplayable dunes beyond. The shrewd play was a driving iron of 210 yards, hit with spin to hold it where it struck; then a pitch or run-up into the tight, mound-collared green.

Junah went for the green off the tee. He didn't want to. But there was Vance, holding out the driver with a look that brooked no possibility of retreat. A thrill coursed through the gallery. So this was how Junah would play it. Five shots back, behind champions who could be expected to pull farther and farther ahead, he had no choice but to go all out. Junah focused. You could see him struggling desperately to relax, to let his grip settle and release the pressure of tension in his fingers. He swung. Not a thing of beauty, but a solid yardage-eating draw. The ball finished just shy of the apron, 270 from the tee; a chip and putt gave him a birdie.

He was gaining. Settling. Twelve was an uphill postage-stamp par three, 170 for the morning round, with the flag hanging slack beneath the mound backing the green. You couldn't feel a breath of breeze; a bank of dunes coupled with the gallery's mass to obscure it where the players stood. There was something moving up there though. A one- or two-club wind, up where an iron would fly. This, as you know, Michael, is what makes club selection so diabolical on a links course; there are no trees, no branches to sway, no way to sense the swirling currents high up. I saw Hagen take out a mashie, the proper club for a shot of 170 without wind. Vance wouldn't bite; he handed Junah a three-iron, which the champion questioned briefly, then knocked stiff for a tap-in deuce. Hagen promptly replaced the mashie and took the club he intended to play all along, a three.

He too birdied. Jones had birdied ten and eleven. For all Junah's heroics, he had regained but a single stroke on his rivals, who now stood tied at two under.

What else was Bagger Vance saying to Junah through these holes? And what did he say now, when momentum could so easily flag and that dire goddess, Collapse, again rear her hideous head?

"Listen to me, Junah. All sport is holy, for it embodies the objectified search for the subjective experience of *yoga*, meaning union, union with the divine. But golf is supreme because it more closely mirrors the Reality of the way to Self-realization. Listen and I will tell you why.

"In other sports the opponent is regarded as the enemy. We seek by our actions to disable him. In tennis our stroke defeats him; in football our tackle lays him low. This is not the way to salvation, or, more accurately, it is at one remove. The golfer on the other hand is never directly affected by his opponent's actions. He comes to realize that the game is not against the foe, but against himself. His little self. That yammering fearful ever-resistant self that freezes, chokes, tops, nobbles, shanks, skulls, duffs, flubs. This is the self we must defeat.

"Consider the golfer's relation to the Rules, Junah. This too differs from every other sport. In baseball a batter, knowing a pitch to be over the plate, will argue vociferously with an umpire to the opposite effect, trying to avoid having a strike called on him. The tennis player will bitterly contest a line call he knows to be fair, the footballer vehemently declare his innocence of a penalty he knows he committed.

"In other words they will lie. Deliberately. To gain selfish advantage.

"It is only in golf, Junah, that players routinely call penalties on themselves. Look at Jones, striding there. Do you remember the '25 Open at Worcester? That great man, your foe this day, lost by a single stroke, the result of his calling a penalty on himself in the first round when his ball moved accidentally. Jones finished tied for first and lost in the play-off. Take away that self-enforced penalty and he would have won outright.

"The greatness of this is that it mirrors Higher Reality. There can be no cheating in the dimension in which the Self resides. There every action inexorably produces its result, every thought its consequence.

"Therefore, Junah, love your opponents. When I say love, I don't mean hand them the match. I mean contend with them to the death, the way a lion battles a bear, without mercy but with infinite respect. Never belittle an opponent in your mind, rather build him up, for on the plane of the Self there can be no distinction between your being and his. Be grateful for your opponents' excellence. Applaud their brilliance. For the greatness of the hero is measured by that of his adversaries. In this too the etiquette and honor of golf reflect the Reality of the Field. Those new to the game often cheer an opponent's misfortune, but the player of wisdom who has entered into the soul of the game schools himself to feel and act the opposite. This too is the greatness of the game.

"But all this you know, Junah. I repeat it now only to focus your distracted mind under this excruciating pressure. To return you to the imperative to act."

Here Junah, who had been listening with as much attention as he could muster under the circumstances, bridled and pulled up in midstride. "I don't understand you, Bagger," he said. "You order me to win, as if I could, but in the same breath you tell me to love my opponents. Please be clear. I need to understand what you're telling me."

"Act, Junah, but act without attachment, as the earth does. As I do. The rain falls, with no thought of watering the land. The clouds roll, not seeking to bring shade. They simply do. And we must too.

"Therefore win, Junah. Hold nothing back. It was not by accident that I told you to hook that ball out of bounds, nor was it chance that made me tell you to hit the drive on ten with all you had.

"We've got Hagen and Jones right where we want them: so far ahead that they leave us no choice but to play all-out. To strike and act without fear or forethought."

"You confuse me again," Junah interrupted. "How can we act without forethought? What you're saying sounds like mystical nonsense! Why did God give us a brain if not to think?"

"Watch and see," Bagger Vance answered calmly. "I will show you the Field and the Knower."

Seventeen

IN THE TWENTIES AND THIRTIES, gallery ropes were rarely in use except around the tees; spectators were permitted to swarm down the fairway alongside the players, constrained from jostling the defenseless competitors only by their own good sense and the beefy shoulders of the occasional marshal. I was caught in such a stampede coming off the thirteenth and swept helplessly away from Vance and Junah. The Field and the Knower. What in the world was *that*? What was Vance telling Junah now? What was he showing him?

I was still a-bob in the maelstrom 150 yards later when I glimpsed, through a gap in the gallery, up ahead as they stood by Junah's ball, Bagger Vance lay a hand on Junah's shoulder. I knew that gesture. Junah seemed to reel under it, a sort of stagger; then his eyes blinked several times, like a man trying to recover focus after a blow. I lost sight of them again as the crush swelled over a rise and then, aided by several spectators who recognized me as part of Junah's party, was able at last to wriggle through into the clear.

I could see Junah up ahead. He was no longer blinking. In his eyes instead was an expression of awe and wonder; he looked drunk or, more accurately, moved. It seemed he might actually weep. What in the world was going on? I wanted to scurry that instant to Bagger Vance's side but Jones, who was away after a drive of 245, was getting set to play. The gallery and I held ourselves motionless as he addressed the ball in his crisp no-nonsense manner, then ripped a beautiful three-iron, cut into the right-to-left wind, onto the putting surface 200 yards distant. I hurried to Junah's ball, which was about ten yards ahead. Junah was staring at Jones, eyes following the master's steps as if hypnotized. "Now watch Hagen," I heard Bagger Vance say quietly, tugging Junah's attention back. "Watch not just his will, but *how* he uses it."

Junah turned obediently toward Hagen, who had a mid-iron in his hands and was stepping aggressively to the ball. The Haig planted his feet, waggled once, checked his line, then slashed a low screamer dead on the stick. Storm clouds had come up over the ocean; the hole spanned a rise unsheltered by the duneline and hard cross-gusts, heralding a blow, whipped erratically across the fairway. Hagen's shot bored beneath them, rising only at the last instant to strike the turf twenty yards short of the green and scamper like a neatly nipped chip onto the surface, curling to rest thirty feet left and long, in perfect position. It was a shotmaker's shot. The gallery showed its knowledge and appreciation with cheers and whistles.

Now it was Junah's turn; the spectators' attention swung

toward him. But his eyes kept following Hagen in awe. He blinked and blinked again, still staring. So intense was Junah's look that it was actually making Hagen uncomfortable; the Haig winked and tipped his hat. This seemed only partially to snap Junah out of it. Vance tugged his elbow and set the bag upright before him. The shot was about 190 into the gusting crosswinds. Junah stepped up quick, set his spikes and cold-topped it. You could hear the blade cut the ball's cover. . . . Ough! It bounded forward like a hot infield grounder, squirting into a bunker a full forty yards short of the green. Junah almost fell over; he looked dizzy and reeling, Vance actually had to steady him with a hand. Junah still didn't move when the gallery surged forward; in moments he was swallowed, standing there, as if dumbstruck.

"What the hell's that damn caddie doing to him now?" I heard Judge Neskaloosa River Anderson in the gallery behind. We pushed our way forward, Vance skillfully running interference for Junah, all the while speaking calmly and instructively into his ear. Observe this. Take notice of that. Junah looked like a man hallucinating. His eyes scanned the sweep of the fairway, becoming mesmerized by something he saw in the sand blowing from a bunker, or the dip of the flag in the wind. Even after his play from the bunker, which he nipped cleanly, finishing on the green just inside Hagen, he still strode in that bedazzled, intoxicated state.

I was getting frightened. Who *was* this Bagger Vance anyway? What powers did he have and how did he come by them? When we reached the green a part of me, fearful, began to hold back. It may have been my imagination, but I was certain that Vance intuited this instantly. He motioned me with a reassuring wave to move beside him.

"Don't be afraid, Hardy," he said when I had crossed the apron and taken a position at his side. "Your role in this is as vital as Junah's."

This *what*? I wanted to ask. But I knew he'd only answer in his cryptic indirect fashion. Hagen was lining up his putt now. Junah stood behind and to the side, ready to learn what he could from the ball's roll.

"Would you like to see what Junah is seeing?" Vance whispered.

A spook ran through me. I knew I had no choice. Then Vance's warm hand was on my shoulder and the bottom blew out of the world.

Lewis Carroll was on to something with the metaphor of stepping through a looking glass. That sense of inversion, of everything being the same and yet its own opposite, that was what it seemed like as, under Vance's hand, I slipped through an invisible membrane and stepped forth into another reality.

As near as I can, I will try to describe what I saw. What Junah had been seeing for the prior five minutes.

The scene itself—fairway, ocean, sky—remained the same. But all laws of color had changed. Grass was no longer green nor heavens blue. Everything shimmered instead with a vibrating chromatic iridescence, including those essences, like air, that we think of as possessing no color at all. More, those vibrations seemed to possess not just life but intelligence. The air had intelligence, the grass had intelligence. The ground beneath my feet appeared not like the planet's surface, but like the shifting bottom of a tropical sea; all currents and creatures became visible in brilliant light-pulsating life. Wind flowed over the land like shimmering rainbow-hued water; the galleries glowed in a mass of hotly vibrating auroras; the turf itself seemed vividly, organically awake. "Behold the Field," I heard Vance's voice, not as if it were speaking to me in reality, but in a dream, from within the dream.

Hagen putted. I watched the ball's path mesmerized, as in the moments before an accident when the world slows down and you look on like a god or a somnambulist, in the world and yet above it. It was a thirty-footer with a double break, to the right down one slope to a flat, then left as it neared the cup. I could see every nuance of the break before the ball was even struck. Force lines, which I felt intuitively to be gravity or some form of supragravity, coursed as visibly as mercury around and down the slopes. It seemed almost redundant when the actual ball took the actual breaks, what seemed like an eternity later. "This is the Field," Bagger Vance's voice came to me from a distance, "you are the Knower." I watched Hagen's ball strobe, just slightly out of alignment with the force flow that hovered inches high along the green, and then his putt ghosted past on the low side. A groan from the gallery, then applause as the ball nestled, a tap-in away.

The next five holes passed in an instant or an eternity, it was impossible to tell which. Vance was instructing Junah by having him watch Jones and Hagen. They understood, he said. They knew how to use the Field.

"Focus your attention on the player's will," Vance instructed

Junah as Jones settled into his stance on the fourteenth tee. "Notice that it is not 'willful.' It is *intentional* but not willful. Do you comprehend the difference?"

This is what Junah saw.

Around Jones, encompassing his body in vibrating concentric fields, spread an aurora of energy. It seemed to *be* his body, but expanded, augmented. It was a field itself. Then there were other fields, an infinitude of them. You could see his will, as Bagger Vance said, his intention *select* the field he chose, which was the fairway and the target line. Lines of force, which were chromatic not just visually but aurally as well, vibrating like music, extended from Jones' intentionality (that's the best I can describe it) down the fairway to the target area. But there were at least two exceptional aspects to this will and to the force lines it apprehended.

First, the force lines seemed to exist outside time, independent of it. And second, they seemed to exert an intentionality of their own.

Let me try to be precise, for this is exceptionally important.

Jones waggled now and set himself over the ball. I saw his swing before he swung it. Much like seeing Hagen's putt before it rolled. But it was not a single swing, as if predetermined; rather it was a number of swings, I would guess a hundred, two hundred, all vibrating simultaneously in Jones' field, as if in alternative futures. Possible futures. They were all recognizably Jones' swing. But some were duffs, tops, skulls, and so on. Bad swings. Now, Michael, this is the interesting part:

I could see Jones' will *search among those swings*, like you or I would hunt through a file drawer for a patient's chart. Jones seemed to settle. To still himself. The auroras surrounding him consolidated. The bad swings fell away, evaporating like a dream; colors intensified around the swings he had intentioned, until there were only half a dozen very closely arrayed swings remaining. As Vance had said, intelligence seemed to pour from Jones' grip, from his hands. Receptive intelligence, searching the Field, drawing from it and upon it. Then Jones swung. In actuality. You could see his motion in the physical dimension track along the motions he had intentioned, not perfectly, but very close to those pre-swings that existed outside of time (or so I felt certain). I was numb, dumbstruck; I couldn't absorb it. The ball rocketed away down the lines of force, with everything humming and glowing and vibrating in some keen cosmic harmony.

Now I knew why Junah had looked drunk. This was too much to take, it was overload. I felt as if my nervous system were about to explode, strained to the maximum to handle the excessive currents coursing along it.

"Know that all that is," Bagger Vance's voice came again as if in a dream, "flows from the union of the Field and the Knower."

"Who *are* you?" I heard myself asking, but my voice seemed to rise with ineffable slowness, as if hallooing up from the bottom of an endlessly deep well. I knew he wouldn't answer. Instead he directed Junah's attention and mine to Hagen, who now teed his ball and stepped to it.

"See how the player's will searches the Field and finds his Authentic Swing." I looked. I saw it, just as Vance said. "Now see him harmonize with it. Not until then does he begin his swing in physicality."

"Are Jones and Hagen seeing this too?" I heard Junah's voice (perhaps only in my head, I couldn't tell) ask Vance.

"Not like you and Hardy are. But yes. In their ways, yes."

Now, Michael, let me address the second phenomenon. I wish I could recall it with more clarity. I wish I had been an adult then, with my physician's training in detached observation. But I was just a boy and I was scared to death. This is the best I can do:

It seemed, watching Hagen as he stood over the ball, as if the process did not consist merely of his selecting from an infinitude of possible swings and possible resulting shots, but that the swing and shot, of their own intelligence, were beckoning to him. A very specific swing and a very specific shot.

The *best* shot.

It was as if before each swing lay an infinitude of futures, every possible way the shot could be struck, and yet pulling stronger than all others was *that which was most excellent*.

Have you seen an eagle soar, Michael? Or watched a shark glide through the water? Don't you sense observing them that each bank of a wing, each trim adjustment of a fin, is its most optimum, its most excellent, the best and finest selection from an infinitude of possibilities? Don't they, the animals, seem closer to God than we? Don't they seem automatically tuned to His will, guided flawlessly by instinct?

Have you ever stood over a putt, Michael, and seen the line laid out as clearly as if it were drawn in chalk on the green? This was something like that.

The optimum, calling to you.

Excellence crying to be brought forth.

This is the best description I can put to it. You could see Hagen's aurora, his intentionality, search the chromatic spectrum—the Field. His vibration stilled, harmonizing with that of the Field, centering in stillness in his chest and his hands. Simultaneously the Field *beckoned* to him; like two frequencies seeking each other in the ether. He wanted to play the best possible shot. And the best possible shot wanted him to play it. Wanted to be brought into physical existence by him. It already existed in some other dimension, but somehow, if you'll permit me to speak in terms so far outside the scientific, *that was not enough for it.* It wanted to exist *here,* on the material plane. And it needed Hagen to make that happen. It needed a person. An embodied soul. A human being.

I wish I could say that I was observing all this in a detached scientific manner. But in fact I was terrified. In a way it was like one's first surgery on a living human being, that first parting of the flesh and beneath it the revelation of another world, a pulsating breathing world that strikes terror in you at the same time that it beckons and fascinates. That was how it felt, only more daunting because I had no training, no preparation. I was just a boy. I felt as if the ground beneath me could no longer be trusted; every physical law was turned on its head. Would I fly up off the earth in defiance of gravity, would I die, was I dead already?

At the same time, it was utterly involving and hypnotic. I dreaded hearing Bagger Vance's voice again, fearful of the mysterious powers he possessed, but at the same time I couldn't wait to hear more. Explain it to me! Tell me what I'm seeing! What in the world is going on here?

The course is the Field, he said, with its vectors, lines of force, tones, colors, harmonies, chromatic and somatic, magnetic lines extending above the earth, along its curvature, up into the stratosphere and soaring off into space, all of it organic and all interconnected. Our bodies were also the Field. This was the holiness of sport: that it opened a pathway via the body to the spirit. He kept instructing Junah in the proper use of the will.

Junah birdied fifteen but bogeyed sixteen. He was overwhelmed; he couldn't get it, it was all too much too fast. Vance continued guiding him quietly but emphatically:

"Hagen and Jones do not will the swing into being, they use their will to *find* the swing that is already there, that was there before they were born and will continue to exist through eternity. Then they surrender their will to it.

"Only when the Knower and the Field are one do they swing.

"The Knowing is everything," Bagger Vance said. "It is the Knowing alone that survives the death of the body. You are your Knowing. The Knowing finds the swing and the swing is you. . . ."

It was somewhere in here that I fainted.

We were on the eighteenth, the final hole of the morning round, when I suddenly became aware that I was on my back on the ground with anxious faces bending over me. I felt my father's cool physician's hands lift me and I knew I had crossed back through the membrane to safety. Already the vision of the other side was fading; I was desperately relieved, grateful as a castaway washed up on dry land, the dislocation was so fearful, and yet I ached for what was already dissolving like a dream.

One fact I knew, even as my head swam and I felt my father lift a cup of cool water to my lips: I knew with every cell of my being that this world, this Field that Vance had somehow revealed to me and Junah, *this* was Reality. The normal world, the everyday consciousness to which I was now so rapidly (and gratefully) returning . . . that was illusion. Or, more accurately, a foreshortened, watered-down version of reality. Reality strained through gauze, diluted and dimmed down to the thinnest of gruels.

This is what I saw at the last.

As the swollen throng surged down the eighteenth, the par five named Valor flush by the ocean, lightning began striking out at sea. The storm was breaking, though I couldn't tell if it was a real storm or the Field crackling with its own voltage, a voltage that was always present but that I—we, in our normal state of awareness—was oblivious to. I felt the charge course from water to land and tingle through the soles of my shoes. Along the beach the lightning strike made a flight of gulls take wing; I saw them in the Field, responding to the Field. They sprung, one following the other, into the air, rowed skyward into formation and wheeled hard toward the west. The flock was the individual, of one mind only, and that mind was wedded intimately to the storm, to the wind, to the currents of finely drawn elemental spirit, strung like filament, which the birds followed flawlessly and without choice.

I had the clearest, most incontrovertible sense that the gulls were *playing*.

This playing was somehow cosmically important.

I sensed that every aspect of the gulls' life, of the storm's life, of the planet's itself, was play. Hunting and killing included. It was all play.

Only we humans broke this natural law.

But we were not breaking it now. We were playing.

This play was, I could see, not in any sense inferior to "work." It was superior. An aspect of devotion, holy in itself, but more than that, absolutely *necessary* in the cosmic scheme. As if the gears of the universe itself depended on these gulls wheeling in the wind and us humans, enmeshed as intimately in that same wind and same Field.

Somehow both playings were equal, perfect and necessary in the sight of God.

I felt an emotion enwrap me, a warmth and sense of safety which I can describe only as sublime. It seemed as if I were on the verge of some great understanding, some holy truth which trembled just beyond the reach of my fingertips.

At the same time I felt I was about to explode. It was too much; there were too many Fields, an infinitude competing for my attention, each tugging my unseasoned mind with its own massive centrifugal power. I whirled among them. My nervous system couldn't take it. I was coming apart, atom by atom. I summoned all my mental power, struggling to return focus to the course, to Junah and the match, but when my vision turned toward the massed gallery the figures dissolved into thousands upon thousands of individual auroras, each and all at once vibrating separately and intertwined, with all their tendrils and filaments brachiating into space, to the Field. . . .

A fuse blew. The circuit breaker snapped open in my head, and I hit the deck, out cold.

Eighteen

THE STORM HAD BROKEN, wind was lashing the medical tent; through the untethered flaps I could see the stampede of galleryites scurrying for shelter as the hard Atlantic rain sheeted in. Is the eighteen over? I kept asking my father. Yes Hardy yes, but you're flushed and fevered, he answered, nestling me firmly onto a camp cot and covering me with a blanket.

"Junah has gone in to the grill for lunch. Jones and Hagen are dining there too, with the press and celebrities and the mucky-mucks."

"Where's Bagger Vance?" I blurted anxiously. Then I saw him, beside the cot, maintaining his usual silent vigil.

"He's here," my father answered, pressing my burning brow and slipping a thermometer beneath my tongue. "He hasn't left your side for a moment."

An hour earlier that news would have been a source of profound reassurance. Now it scared the bejesus out of me. I didn't want Vance to touch me. Not that hand again on my shoulder! I couldn't stand any more unscheduled flights to the ozone. But here was Vance moving beside me; I could see his huge strong hands. "May I, Dr. Greaves?" he asked my father, meaning could he examine me in his own fashion. Before I could stammer a protest, my dad had nodded and Vance was lifting me gently to a sitting posture.

"The body is also a Field," Vance spoke softly, for my ears alone, "known by the hands of the lover . . . the athlete . . . and the physician." His fingertips tapped me three times—once on each word, each tap higher on the spine—then rapped me one final pop on the crown of the head. A rush of energy shot from my tailbone straight out the top of my skull. I would have passed out again, had Vance's hand not steadied me.

Then, in a flash, I was fine.

My father plucked the thermometer. "Ninety-eight point six," he announced with surprise and relief. "There's no tonic like youth for a quick recovery!"

I was given a hot shower and dry clothes. Junah brought a meal for me from the grill, hot brunswick stew with bean salad and hush puppies which I ate with my dad and the shoeshine boys, straddling a bench in the players' locker room.

Junah himself had gone on to the club storage room. I followed forty-five minutes later, as soon as my father would let me.

The room was empty. Brand new and gleaming, with its freshly carpentered golf-bag racks, row after row from floor to ceiling, each brass-numbered slot smelling of freshly cut lumber and all of them vacant, waiting for the first hotel guests.

Junah sat motionless on the floor, eyes closed, crosslegged like a Sioux, with Bagger Vance in an identical pose directly opposite.

The sight made me even more agitated. What mesmeric snare had Vance caught Junah in now? What bizarre scenario was playing out *now* in the champion's mind? As if reading my thoughts, Vance opened his eyes and turned to me.

"We are practicing, Hardy," he said softly so as not to disturb Junah. "We have worked through the woods and mid-irons. We'll finish with niblicks and sand shots, then a little putting."

I peered. Junah's clubs were all in the bag.

"We have no need of clubs"—Vance again spoke before I could—"in many ways they are an impediment."

He declared that the exercise Junah was now performing was a primeval discipline of sport—sport, he emphasized, which contrary to contemporary wisdom had not evolved from the arts and skills of war, but in fact preceded them. "Did you know that the philosophers and *rishis* of the Indus Valley played an ancient form of golf? They played without clubs or balls. They were the greatest shotmakers who ever lived!"

I was running out of patience with this stuff. Maybe it was the cold, or my irritation with the rain delay; maybe my fear for my own self and how Vance so easily toyed with my mind; maybe I was afraid for Junah, who had become as dear to me as a brother over the past eighteen holes.

"I'll bet they were," I responded hotly, "and you were probably there too. One of the reechies."

"*Rishis,*" Vance corrected me gently. "And no, I was not one
of them." He paused. "I taught them."

"Of course. You were the pro! Twenty-one thousand years
ago." I warmed to the sarcasm. "Or was it twenty-one million?
When Krewe Island was called Mu."

"See," Vance said with a grin, "you *are* learning."

I was getting madder and madder. I remembered what Vance
had said about the battle, the one that had been fought here at
Krewe Island, and I began to mock that with my best ten-year-
old's scorn when Junah suddenly released a profound inner moan
and began to rise, still entranced, from his seated posture.

I broke off, staring. Junah rose gracefully, unconscious as a
sleepwalker, and began slowly to glide through a series of poses.
The Krewe Island bath towel that had been draped over his
shoulders now fell, revealing his bare back. I gasped at the sight
of his war-scarred flesh. Lurid welts that could only be bullet
wounds rose in knotted knobs beneath his shoulder blades. Two
striated slashes that my boy's imagination credited to some kind
of blade or bayonet spanned the width of his lower back. His
whole left upper torso was a mottled moonscape of third-degree
burn scars. This of course had become invisible to him. In the
trance, his spine arched forward and back, he twisted and canted.
Vance watched casually but with keen attention, as if he were
monitoring by some mysterious process Junah's every thought
and vision.

"This posture you see Junah entering now is called, in the East, *Dandahan Virasana*. Chariot Warrior pose."

Junah balanced with legs spread, hips low and spine erect, arms extended, joined powerfully in a single grip.

"*Danda* in Sanskrit means 'weapon.' *Han* is 'strike.' Together with *vira*, 'hero,' they are translated by the moderns as 'warrior.' But *danda* in the primordial Vedic meant not 'weapon' but 'club.' And *han* to the ancients was without exception 'swing.'

"In other words," he said, " 'warrior' was originally 'swinger of the club.' "

This fellow is making a fool of me and *Junah*, I thought. I became furious. I was ready to blast him with my highest indignation, when Junah, still deep in transport, began to glide anew. Hands yoked with unfaultable grace, he executed, first to the right and then to the left, a flawless golf swing!

At this precise instant, a sharp rapping banged from the door. "Mr. Junah," Dougal McDermott's voice came through the pine, "are ye in thaer, sir?" Junah wove woozily back to consciousness. The pro's head popped into view with a smile. "Storm's clearin', sir. Will ye be ready soon? Mr. Jones an' Mr. Hagen are preparin' tae move tae th' practice tee."

Junah stood, blinking, still half in trance. Vance answered. "I'll come with you now, Mr. McDermott. These irons need to be emery-clothed and I must mink-oil Mr. Junah's spare shoes. He will follow shortly."

He whispered a few words to Junah, then shouldered the bag and moved off behind McDermott.

I turned to Junah.

We were alone.

"Are you all right, sir?" Concern and emotion flooded my voice. "What is that man doing to you?!"

"Who?" Junah blinked. "McDermott?"

"No—Vance! Your caddie, if indeed that's what he is!"

Junah straightened and brought his eyes into focus. "Why? Are you worried?" He was completely unruffled, gathering several balls and tees, ready to follow in Vance's wake to the lockers.

"Who *is* he?" I caught the champion's sleeve. "You have to tell me, Mr. Junah! Is he a demon? Or some kind of fakir who spellbinds us into trances?"

Junah laughed gaily. "How does a sprig like you know a word like *fakir*?"

"I'm not stupid," I responded indignantly. "I read books. My father's a doctor, and I'm gonna be one too!"

"Not a golf pro?" he teased.

"Heck no! I'm gonna be like you and Bobby Jones, an amateur. And win the U.S. Open!"

"My, my. A doctor *and* an Open champ."

He was deflecting me off the subject, just like Vance did. It made me even angrier.

"You have to tell me who this fellow is! How does he make us see these crazy visions? And that way he talks. Every time he puts his hand on my shoulder, more cracked stuff keeps happening!"

"On your shoulder? You mean like this?" Junah lunged teasingly toward me; I sprang backward. He began laughing in earnest.

I was upset and scared. Junah could see it. He motioned me over kindly and made me take a seat on the bench beside him.

"Don't be afraid, Hardy. Whatever Vance is, he will never harm you. In fact, I'll make you a promise: as long as he stands beside you, no harm can come to you from any quarter."

"But who *is* he? Where did you meet him? How can he do the things he does?"

"Why don't you ask him?"

"Because he never gives a straight answer! And you're pulling the same trick!"

I felt Junah's arm wrap warmly around my shoulder. His eyes met mine; he tugged me gently to him like a brother. "Let me ask you something, Hardy." His tone had become serious. "What you and I saw out there on the course this morning, what Bagger Vance allowed us to see . . . what do you think is its relation to Reality?"

I knew what he was going to say. That it *was* Reality. That the world we see normally, our everyday world, is nothing but . . .

"I've seen that Reality before." Junah's words cut off my thought. "Shall I tell you where?"

His tone sent a shiver through me.

"In France."

He meant the Great War. My spine went to ice; I felt the hair stand straight up on my neck.

"That is where I met Vance. Stepping forth from a cloud of

shellfire to preserve me. He was my driver. Or rather, became my driver."

Junah broke off for a moment, absent in memory. Then his glance returned and focused on me.

"I was in a veterans hospital for most of a year," the champion spoke softly, "upon my return from England after the armistice. My mind had slipped its moorings, as they say. I was lost upon the storming inner oceans, quite insane according to the doctors. Vance never left me. He was my guide and instructor."

"Instructor in what?" I demanded, becoming even more agitated.

"He started me playing golf again. That was when he made Schenectady Slim."

"What? Vance *made* that driver?"

"From a hickory bough he brought from the woods beneath my window. The hospital was in Schenectady, New York."

Junah met my eyes and held them. "When my inner world was careening off its axis, Vance would place my hands in a grip upon that driver. It never failed to quell my terror. I was able to be tossed upon those inner seas and not be driven mad."

Junah stopped and glanced up. Bagger Vance stood there. He had slipped back soundlessly through the door and now glided forward, bringing Junah a dry, oiled pair of golf shoes. "The human being at his current level," Vance spoke softly, directly to me, "is incapable of perceiving Reality, except in rare ecstatic bursts. In earlier eras, men could hold that consciousness longer. In future ages, they will again. But not now. That is what golf is for."

He asked if I understood; I said no.

"Are you afraid, Hardy?" he spoke gently. "If you'd rather not continue with us . . ."

"No . . . no!" I blurted. Unexpected emotion came rushing over me. To my surprise I realized I didn't care who Vance was or what dark forces tormented Junah; all I knew was I couldn't stand to be anywhere except with them. The thought of being separated from them, held even for a moment in my imagination, was enough to plunge me into despair.

Was Vance some kind of dervish who had mesmerized me into his power? He must be, or why was I so desperate to stay? Why was I so certain that Vance knew every thought that had flashed through my mind just now and every thought I had had since the moment we met?

I watched him kneel before Junah, helping the champion slip into his fresh spikes. Vance snugged the shoes over Junah's dry socks and began to lace them up.

"By the way, Hardy"—he grinned at me over his shoulder—"have you heard the morning's scores? Our man came in in 35 for a far-from-shameful 76. Hagen's at 70, Jones at 69."

Nineteen

A T THIS POINT in the telling of the story, Michael and I
became aware of a storm breaking—a real one, just like
the storm in the story—smack outside across the inlet. We could
see lightning flash over Skidaway Island and hear the willows in
the yard moan in the rising wind. It was past ten o'clock, both of
us were getting restless; we were debating braving the weather
for a hike down the beach, when I suddenly remembered:

"My goodness, Michael, something just occurred to me. I
don't know how I could have forgotten: Junah's granddaughter
is here! Now, in Savannah. On Skidaway Island."

"His granddaughter?"

"The daughter of the young child he left in Germany. Do you
remember? When his wife died and he returned to the States in
'27? She's long since a grown woman, in her thirties now, I believe. How could it have slipped my mind? I've been in contact
with her, making arrangements to return certain books which

Junah left me in his will. No doubt that's why he's been so much on my mind of late, and why I was inspired to tell his tale to you tonight."

Junah's granddaughter and her husband made their home in Boston, I told Michael, but they kept a cottage out on the island. Did he think it was too late to phone—and possibly drive over?

The young lady's married name was Lederer. Irene Lederer. I had her phone number from correspondence we had exchanged. But should we call? She had small children and no doubt could use her sleep. It was Michael who insisted; perhaps this was serendipity, at least it was inspiration. "Besides, you called on her grandfather once at a late hour, and that seemed to be blessed by fortune."

We phoned. Irene was up. We drove over. The storm had become a real Atlantic rattler. Shrimpers were bobbing at their moorings as we passed the Skidaway basin; rain was blowing in sheets across the causeway. I was encouraged that Michael wanted to meet Junah's granddaughter and yet, in the dimness of my clattering Dodge's front seat, I could feel his mood, brooding and dark. He seemed to sense my unease and spoke: "Dr. Greaves, I appreciate what you're trying to do for me tonight. Believe me, it means a lot, just that you would take the time. I wish I could say it was helping."

Anyone who has watched a child grow to adulthood knows the peculiar sensation, a kind of multiple perception that doubles our vision of him as a grown-up. It becomes impossible not to see him still in short pants and muddy T-shirt. I realized as

I glanced at Michael now in the storm, in the dimness of the dash-lit seat, that I was still seeing him as that carefree young caddie with the pure natural grip and the faultless free-flowing swing. How had he grown into this troubled young man, to these same torments that had plagued Junah, and myself as well, for so many years?

Michael was, Junah included, the finest student-athlete ever to come out of Savannah. Universities as far away as Harvard and Berkeley had courted him since eighth grade; he chose Penn, where he was Academic All-American in football, basketball and track and a scratch golfer almost as an afterthought. He possessed that rarest combination of athletic gifts, the speed and power of a track star with the hand and eye coordination of a billiard master. I watched him one afternoon pick up a lacrosse stick for the first time; within an hour there was no player on the field, including two All-Americans, who could defend him. But these gifts, rather than flushing Michael with confidence and self-assurance, seemed only to trouble and torment him. Like a woman blessed with spectacular beauty, he was profoundly mistrustful of the effect his presence produced so effortlessly on other people.

The fact that Michael was black I am sure only added to the dubiousness with which he regarded his gifts. He refused to be stereotyped either as an athlete or a scholar. I think it may have been the excessive attention he received in other sports that drew Michael so powerfully to golf. His admirers all thought him a fool. There was no big payday coming from golf, no signing bonus or Super Bowl incentive clause. I myself observed Michael's passion with deep satisfaction. As I told him earlier in the evening, I sensed that he saw through to the soul of the game. Golf kept Michael humble, and I think that meant a great deal to him. Many times watching him grow, I was almost eerily reminded of Junah. Here was that same instinct for the game, the same grace and power. What a shame he and Junah could never have met. That, I suppose, was at least partly what I hoped to redress this evening. To give Michael a flesh-and-blood sense of that other tortured athlete, that other brilliant product of Savannah's tidal shores.

I was failing. Michael withdrew into silence, uneasy, and even, I sensed, a bit guilty. I was at a loss and didn't know how to continue.

"When you talk of war," Michael broke the silence, "of Junah's mental torment . . . and I know you suffered too in your own war. I mean, on the one hand I empathize with your pain and all that you both went through. . . ." He broke off, then continued with sudden emotion: "But the truth is I *envy* you." He stopped again; I glanced across at him. "This body God gave me, these talents. I know it sounds crazy but I feel like I am a warrior, like these gifts I've been given were meant for that, for battle. Not battle in the modern sense of push buttons and machines, but something ancient and noble, hand to hand, with ringing steel. And yet . . ."

His voice broke off. I was about to prompt him when he turned, peered out at the storm and resumed. "And yet I know exactly what Junah meant when he had Bagger Vance drive him away that day onto the duneland. How can anyone of consciousness fight willingly in war? How could I—for all the skill I'm sure I'd have at it? I've marched in demonstrations, Dr. Greaves, I've stood across picket lines from men and women who hated me. But I . . . I couldn't hate them. I didn't hate them. If it were war, could I kill them? They were just me. Me with another man's face. It wasn't *real,* do you know what I mean? The battle. In a way I thought studying Medicine would give me that. Life and death. Real actions taken for real people. But . . ." Michael's voice trailed off. "You know what that's like."

We drove on for several minutes, across the Neskaloosa and onto the old barge road that paralleled the Intracoastal Waterway. Michael was relating with frustration his experiences in medical school, the relentless pressure toward specialization, the overriding pursuit of the dollar, the contempt for patients that oozed from the pores of so many of his fellow students and instructors. I felt a terrible sense of futility; it was clear that my efforts were not communicating what I had hoped. I found myself thinking of ancient Greece, which had become, for its troubling parallels with our own time, more and more a preoccupation of mine. The so-called Golden Age lasted only three generations. Junah's was our first generation, the first of our American Golden Age. Mine was the second; Michael's now the third. In Athens Junah's and mine would have been the gallant decades of Aeschylus and Sophocles, Pericles and Themistocles; ours would have been the glories of Marathon and Thermopylae, Salamis and Artemisium. Michael's would have been the bitter third generation of Alcibiades, the generation of plague and empire when painted youth mocked the Mysteries and fell from the excess of their own brilliance.

This is what I feared for Michael. That his generation, so strong, so well made, so bright and aware beyond its years, would compare itself to us in envy, envy of the clarity of our challenges and the brutish obviousness of our enemies. What was I trying to tell him? That to us when it was happening, it hadn't been so clear, it hadn't been so obvious. The world had looked much as it did to him now, a hellish twilight era with greatness fled and meaning elusive as sand between our fingers. My mood became as dark as the storm. I was just glancing over to Michael, not even sure what I was going to say, when he suddenly lunged past me and seized the steering wheel. "Look out!" The car swerved wildly under his grasp; I turned in shock as our hurtling mass blew past a homeless man, standing in the roadway! "Sonofabitch!" Michael shouted in anger at the fellow, eyes flashing rearward. I had the wheel now; we bucked and twisted back onto the pavement. "Are you all right?" Michael asked, his voice shaking.

"Yes, yes, I'm fine. We didn't hit him, did we?"

No, Michael assured me. In the mirror I could glimpse the man gliding on, vanishing without haste into the tall grass. Michael glared back through the rain. "What the hell's the matter with these people? Jesus! That bastard was right in the middle of the road!"

We were delayed for an oil barge at the drawbridge onto Skidaway. Had the rain not been so thick and had we been able to mount the bridge's towers, we could have peered east toward the linksland that had once been Krewe Island. What was left of Invergordon's ancient acreage was now a wildlife preserve, only four or five miles away; not far in fact from the spot where we had nearly hit the derelict man. I could see Michael was still upset by the incident. We sat in a line of cars with their wipers beating and steam rising from their hot idling engines.

Michael spoke: "Did I ever tell you about the trip my family took to New York City, when I was eleven?" I was so relieved to hear him speak that I put all I could into my encouraging reply. Michael turned toward me and relaxed somewhat in his seat. "My dad carried us up there on Amtrak, to see the Statue of Liberty and the U.N. He wanted to show us our legacy as Americans. The sights of course made practically no impression on me. What struck me, and has stayed with me to this day, was an event that happened purely by chance—one midnight, when we found ourselves marooned in Times Square. We were coming from some show on Broadway and couldn't get a cab to pick us up. My mom and brothers were hungry so we stopped in one of those sidewalk Orange Julius places. My father, I realize now, was feeling helpless and furious, but I was young and completely oblivious. I stayed outside on the sidewalk, alone, mesmerized by the passing multitudes. They were of every age and sex, every race and color, streaming past beneath the neon. I had never seen such grotesque or tormented-looking specimens. Each seemed immersed in his own private hell, driven by demons only he or she could name. I was seized with an overwhelming sense of pity. I wanted to rush out among those warped and misbegotten forms and embrace each person one by one and somehow, by magic or instinct or just by wishing it so hard it had to come true, make them well again. Restore them. Make them clean and straight. I would have given anything . . . everything . . . for that gift."

Michael's voice trailed off in sorrow; his dark eyes glanced across to me. "Later, in medical school, we studied palpation with a Bengali doctor named Gupta. He was blind, or nearly so, but he had the most beautiful hands I'd ever seen. He would put them on his patients without any of the hesitation or self-consciousness of a Western doctor. The thing he impressed upon us was always to use two hands. If you were palpating with your right, keep your left on the patient as well. It comforts them, he said. Listen with your right hand, put love in with your left. Of course my classmates snickered like hell at that." Michael's voice broke off again, and when I looked across in the dimness his eyes as well were turned away.

It was almost eleven when we got to Irene Lederer's cottage, tumbling in in a welter of wet shoes and sodden jackets. I apologized at once for the lateness; could she forgive us for thrusting our presence upon her at this hour? "Don't be silly," the young lady insisted, "I wouldn't have invited you over if I didn't mean it. Come in, come in, we're all wide awake anyway. No one on the whole island's going to get any sleep in this storm."

Irene's children were in pajamas, her three and two from the neighbor's, all with various coughs and sniffles but generally just using the storm as an excuse to stay up. Irene and two teenage nieces had them settled campsite-style in sleeping bags around the fireplace. When I introduced Michael it created a stir; the girls all knew of him; he was a hero; he had to endure a grilling on the subject of why he had turned down a draft from the Atlanta Falcons after graduation. Irene brought coffee and we settled onto cozy couches around the fire.

Irene herself was an exceptionally handsome woman in her mid-thirties, quite tall, with much of her grandfather in her. She had his fine high forehead and keen gray eyes. But what struck me most were her hands, which were virtual duplicates of Junah's: the same long slender fingers, same strength and beauty. She even gestured with them much as he had. Junah had had a particularly appealing cock-legged stance when he was listening intently to something, with his head canted to favor his right ear and his hands deep in his pockets. "You stand in that exact posture," I told her. I asked about her mother, Junah's daughter, and Irene said she was in Pacific Grove, California, now, doing research on migratory butterflies. Irene's husband Jim was in Boston, planning on coming down in a week.

Irene and I lamented the fact that we had never found time, or made time, to make each other's acquaintance and discuss her grandfather. She had never known him but had heard many tales from her mother. "It's hard to get an objective picture from a daughter, you know? I could never tell how much of what Mom said was real and how much was pure hero worship."

"Dr. Greaves has been telling me about your grandfather all night," Michael addressed Irene. "I wish you had been there to hear it. We're in the middle of 36 holes with Bobby Jones and Walter Hagen."

Judging by the three reweighted sand wedges stacked in the corner, Irene was something of a golfer herself, as I knew her mother had been, and she jumped at the prospect of hearing more about her grandfather. "Let me listen in for the second eighteen," she volunteered. "Have I missed too much to make sense of it?"

I wasn't convinced that now was the time or place to continue. She and Michael insisted however, seconded by the children, who with cups of cocoa clearly intended to take advantage of this rare excursion into the wee hours.

I did my best to bring them all up to date quickly. Irene was aware of the 1931 match and even produced an album with clippings and later correspondence between her grandfather and Jones. I found myself, as I told the tale in abbreviated form, deliberately softening the parts about Bagger Vance's powers, no doubt from fear of Irene's incredulity. Surprisingly she became impatient with my vagueness and asked several times specifically to know more about the fellow. "My mother talked about him all the time, and my grandfather's writings are full of him. He vanished after the match, didn't he? Do you have any idea what became of him?"

I told her I didn't, with the exception of one rather mysterious occasion which perhaps would weave itself into this tale as it unfolded. Should I continue? I was ready to pick up where we left off, at the start of the second eighteen, when Michael spoke up.

"You ask what became of Bagger Vance," he addressed Irene, then hesitated. "Perhaps I shouldn't inquire at this point, but can you tell me, what happened to your grandfather? After the match, I mean. What did he do? Did his life change?"

Irene glanced once to me, almost as if asking permission to answer. She could see Michael's curiosity burning, perhaps because that issue—what to do with one's life—was so much on his mind at that moment.

"One thing I know for sure," Irene began. "Immediately after the match he returned to Germany to collect my mother, who was five or six at the time. He brought her back to the States along with her grandmother who was raising her and settled them with him at the Aerie. From what my mother told me growing up, my grandfather absolutely devoted himself to her from then on. That, and his passion for navigation."

Michael leaned forward at this. "Navigation?"

"My grandfather developed the first aircraft guidance system that wasn't dependent on celestial, magnetic or gyroscopic orientation. It was called Polar Antivalence Navigation. I don't know how technical you want me to get, but antivalence bases its guidance processes on—"

Michael broke in: "Lines of force. The fields of subtle energy surrounding the earth."

"Yes, that's it. How did you know?"

Michael didn't answer, just glanced once, very quickly, in my direction. "Please go on," he continued to Irene. "What exactly was your grandfather working on?"

"Don't get me started," Irene smiled. "I'm afraid I've become a bit obsessed with it myself, at least as it applies to music." Michael and I had noted in the rear of the cottage a big under-construction studio packed with computer and synthesizer gear, along with ancient intruments, viols, lyres and theorbos.

"My grandfather was fascinated by the significance of vibration, frequencies, harmonics. He believed that surrounding the earth were numerous 'flows' and 'meridians' of energy, like magnetic fields but infinitely subtler, which could be used in navigation if we could develop instruments sensitive enough to detect them. He claimed that Nature herself already did. In a brain as tiny as a butterfly's. He kept birds, hundreds of them. Migratory waterfowl. He had a regular wildlife refuge at the Aerie. The birds, he said, navigate along those subtle flows, and our planes could too."

Here Irene's handsome features grew darker. "My grandfather, as Dr. Greaves may have told you, was obsessed with the coming World War. He felt America must be ready and take up fascism's challenge early and forcefully. This was not a popular belief at that time. My grandfather had become a flier by then, for his navigation research, and he tangled with Charles Lindbergh who as you know was a passionate isolationist, an America Firster. I'm afraid my grandfather came out on the short end of that stick."

Irene was getting agitated. She shifted in her seat, then, rousing herself with a smile, asked how our coffee was holding up. Did we need a warm-up? She was on her feet now. "But please,"

she called back as she moved to the kitchen, "don't let my ram-
blings tear us away from the story. I know that much of my
grandfather's subsequent life sprung directly from the events of
that day at Krewe Island. Please go on, Dr. Greaves. Tell us
what happened on the second eighteen."

Twenty

J UNAH AND VANCE headed for the first tee again.

The rain had stopped at least an hour earlier, but with draining and cleanup, bailing of the bunkers and the dispatching of crews with their twenty-foot bamboo whisks to whip the water off the greens, not to mention the players' warm-up, another hour and a half had been consumed. It was past 3:00 before the officials declared the turf playable and almost 3:30 by the time the competitors shook hands again and finished obliging the relentless importunities of the news photographers. Would there be time to finish? Sunset was at 7:06, which should have allowed more than sufficient margin, though the marshals feared that the gallery, in the muck, could become unruly. But the wind was working strong at ground level, drying the fairways, and the linksland's excellent drainage provided additional cause for optimism. All would be dry, it was hoped, by the turn and more than playable, if a bit damp, till then.

On the tee, Adele Invergordon thanked the galleryites for their patience, requested their forbearance amid the sloppy conditions and introduced Dougal McDermott to reconvene the competition. Junah had reagitated himself terrifically in the previous five minutes. Finishing the warm-up, he tugged Bagger Vance aside. "I can't take any more of these mental fireworks. You have to give me something concrete. One simple thought, just to get my swing started."

"As you wish, Junah," Vance immediately acquiesced. Relief! You could see the tension drain from Junah. He moved in closer to his caddie as they started, amid the gallery, toward the tee.

"Every great player," Vance said, "no matter how odd or unorthodox his swing, shares one crucial consciousness: an absolute awareness of the clubhead at all points in the swing. Jones achieves this with rhythm, Hagen with his hands and his timing. Your key, Junah, is your arc."

This was true. As soon as Junah heard it, a tumbler seemed to snick blessedly into place in his brain.

"Under pressure," Vance continued, "you tend to constrict your arc, as if you imagined that compactness would equate to control. Nothing could be more misguided. Under pressure, *extend* your arc. Let the clubhead go wide; *then* you'll feel it. That's why I keep telling you to hit hard, hold nothing back. Think of this over the ball, Junah: start wide and stay wide. Extend, extend, extend."

This was the exact tonic Junah needed. Something clean. Something simple. You could see the confidence flow into him as he and Vance climbed the rise to number one tee.

The gallery was much diminished from the morning. What had been ten thousand, I would guess, was down to a third of that. This was still a prodigious mob to follow only one threesome, but contrasted with the hordes of the morning it felt almost intimate. Faces were becoming familiar. You knew that these, out again in the wet, were the diehards, the true lovers of the game.

This had a decidedly stabilizing effect on Junah. He joked easily with Hagen and Jones, scraping wet clumped grass from his spikes with a tee, then hip-hopping a ball up and down on the face of his driver.

"Gentlemen"—McDermott's gesture swept down the open fairway—"play away!"

Number one was the straightaway par five that Junah had bogeyed in the morning round. (On the opening four, if you recall, he had fallen five behind.) Hagen was up first and ripped a beauty down the left side that bounced once, flung a plug of wet turf and dropped dead around 245. Jones followed, a little stiffly, with a rolling draw that hit with overspin and squirted forward on the damp grass, stopping close enough to Hagen's that you could have covered both balls with a blanket. The hole was only 521, well within reach for any of the three, except for a sculpted 30-yard swale that crossed the fairway just in front of the green. Vance had had me trot out earlier to inspect this, so we knew there was runoff in the ditch; it had become a small "burn" as they say in Scotland, a stream crossing linksland to the ocean. In this muck a spoon shot aimed at the green, even after a drive of 260, would have to carry all the way, and that probably from a gloppy lie with mud on the ball.

Junah switched from a driver to a driving iron off the tee. The gallery let out a murmur of surprise and, from the Savannah contingent, disappointment. Their man was playing safe, they concluded. Trying just to hold on, bunt it around, keep within ten or twelve strokes and not disgrace himself too badly. I confess that was what I thought too. There was a collective sigh, and then Junah drilled a conservative shot down the right side, catching a downslope about 220 and skittering forward another 10 yards to a flat dry area on the edge of the fairway. From there a solid mid-iron put him about 80 yards short, on the flat before the ditch. An easy pitch to about 15 feet, a putt that burned the right edge and he had his par. Jones and Hagen took the same.

"Why isn't he ripping it?" I asked Bagger Vance as we crossed to the second tee. The caddie kept striding. "He's a shot better than he was this morning, isn't he?"

Now, slowly, it began to happen. I know you've experienced the same, Michael and Irene, on a day when you go around a course twice. At each tee you can't help but recall your morning score for that hole, and the sorrier it was, the more you're inspired by the room for improvement. You know you can't do worse, so you let it rip!

Surely this was what Junah felt on the second tee, remembering his bogey from the morning. He drilled another driving iron, a clean 220 to a dry level lie, then punched a niblick under the wind to six feet. The slower green took some of the break away; the ball tumbled in on the low side. Birdie. He had bettered this morning's score on the hole by two shots. An improvement of three already, in just two holes! You could see Junah gather yet more confidence. Simply matching the morning round the rest of the way would give him 73. For the two rounds, 76-73. Damn good for a soul thrown at the last instant into a battle of titans. Hagen and Jones had both parred two, so Junah had the honor on three. He had picked up a shot.

Junah parred three and four, with Hagen bogeying the fourth when he left an uphill putt short and lipped out from three feet. Junah had gained another on Hagen, to within four, though Jones was still an insuperable six ahead with fourteen holes left.

And Jones was playing superbly. Well within himself, swinging smoothly and full of confidence. His driver, Jeannie Deans as it was called, seemed incapable of striking a ball off-line, and each time Calamity Jane set down on a putting surface, first before the ball then behind it, you were sure Jones would drain it. On all four holes he had scorched the lip from beyond fifteen feet. These burners were sure to start falling sooner or later.

A break came in the opposite direction at number five when Jones, straining to cut the dogleg, plugged his drive into the face of a bunker and took two to get out. Double bogey to Hagen's and Junah's pars.

Suddenly Junah was within four.

I saw him look to Bagger Vance then. We were on the sixth tee and there was no doubt what the glance meant. He wanted to see the Field. Vance grinned, with a teasing glint.

"Think you can handle it now? Yes! *Now* your will is engaged. Now you *want* the prize."

"Isn't that what I'm supposed to want?" Junah whispered back, somewhat shaken by Vance's teasing tone. "Isn't that what you told me?"

"All I want is that you swing your Authentic Swing."

Junah let out a breath, frustrated. "Please don't confuse me again, Bagger. I thought you wanted me to *win*."

"I couldn't care less about winning," the mysterious fellow answered. "I care about *you*."

He put his hand on Junah's shoulder.

Junah knew what was coming.

It did.

This time Vance did not ask me to share the vision; I remained on the outside, watching Junah much as a sober man may observe a drunk.

"We are speaking of a State of Grace," Vance told Junah as they squinted up this gale-swept 230-yard par three, "which is by definition an aspect of the divine. You have blundered through this portal in the past, by my assistance and by happy accident, as every golfer has. Now observe it with eyes open. Learn from it. . . ."

Junah seemed to stagger under this weight for a long moment; then, slowly, he found his feet and settled in.

Then came the stroke of the match, to that point.

The shot Junah hit, a drilled driver, unteed, cut into that stiff right-to-left gale, was beyond anything any of the players had yet attempted, let alone pulled off. Let me describe it briefly, as it remains one of the three or four greatest shots I have ever seen.

The sixth was uphill, 230 as I said, with the ocean hard by on the right, across the short beach above a bluff. In the morning with the wind behind, all three players had hit driving irons; now, with the gale hammering into their faces, the hole played a full four clubs longer. The cup, which had been recut for the afternoon round, was perched at the extreme right, practically teetering on the bluff edge, with the wind bowing the flagstick thirty degrees over and making the fabric of the flag snap like a pistol shot. Getting close was out of the question. The only way even to strike the putting surface, if your nerves were steel, was to start the ball twenty or thirty yards out over the breakers and let the wind take it back. The problem was the long carry; it called for a full driver, which couldn't be spun at all off a tee; by the time the gale-borne shot drifted back, what little spin it had would have been killed by the wind; it would plummet like a knuckleball and bound inevitably over the fast-drying green into the murderous bunker protecting the left—the same bunker Junah had had to play backward out of in the morning round. The smart shot was a bail-out, with a spoon or a driving iron, to the fairway short and left, relying on an up-and-down from seventy or eighty feet to make par. That was what Jones did, playing first. The gallery applauded his shrewd, immaculately struck shot. Hagen had a spoon in hand and was clearly intending to play with the same prudence.

Junah took Schenectady Slim. He set the ball cold on the turf, without a tee, and ripped a screamer that started out for the extreme right edge, the bluff edge, of the green. The wind pounded mercilessly from the right. But Junah had given the shot a hard solid cut, *into* the gale. The gallery watched, mesmerized, as the spun ball burrowed its nose dead into the wind's teeth. It rose and held. Straight . . . straight . . . with the wind killing its momentum more and more, exactly as Junah had envisioned, till the driver, which without the gale would have carried twenty or thirty yards over, ran out of steam at precisely the right point, dead above the stick, and dropped as light as a leaf to the putting surface. The angle kicked it sideways another ten feet, where it curled to a stop a flag-length below the hole.

Hagen and Jones reacted as if struck a physical blow. This was not the shot of an amateur. Not a Trans-Miss level shot, not a Georgia State champion shot. It was as good as anything the two giants could have hit themselves on their best day, and maybe better. When Junah coolly rolled in his deuce, the match shifted upward to another gear.

Now that driving iron off the first took on a new significance. The gallery sensed it. Junah had not played chicken. It was not a give-up shot but a deliberate play of patience, the confidence of knowing there were plenty of holes left, nothing had to be rushed so early.

Now was the time to make a move, and now Junah made it.

On seven, with the honor, he teed a spoon and drilled a flawless draw a hundred yards past the bunker over which he had sniped his drive out of bounds in the morning round. The ball lit in a neck no wider than eight yards between two strings of pot bunkers, setting up an easy lofter approach which, the spectators sensed, he would stiff for another birdie.

A thrill began to build in the gallery. Junah's play was a gaunt-

let thrown down to Hagen and Jones. Still of course they anticipated his collapse. No amateur at his level, however lucky he
might be on a given shot or even two or three, could expect to
sustain that rarefied plateau over twelve more grueling holes.
Junah would crash. He would crumble. But meanwhile, Jones
and Hagen had to be thinking, the gallery had witnessed this fellow pull off a couple of blows that were beyond anything they,
Jones and Hagen, had so far even attempted.

It ignited them.

Hagen took a driver off seven and powdered it thirty yards
past Junah's brilliant spoon, into a slot even narrower and closer
to the green. Jones saved his genius for the approach, drilling a
gorgeous side-spinning pitch into the left-to-right slope and curling it down to three feet, dead below the hole.

Vance had now backed away from Junah. His monologue
ended; the caddie no longer poured a stream of inspiration into
his champion's ear. They only grunted to each other on the seventh green; a nod from Vance and Junah stroked his twelve-
footer dead into the cup.

Who can say by what mysterious process news spreads over a
golf course? The battle had been joined, and now the tom-toms
began to boom. Fresh recruits swelled the gallery. Cars that had
been departing suddenly pulled over along the muddy roadsides,
their occupants hiking back to get in on the action. Others who
had taken refuge in various grills and dining rooms now forsook
these havens and braved the elements afresh. Still others, whose
plan had been to stake out premium positions on the closing

holes, now rethought their strategy. They abandoned their prize vantages and began trekking the holes in reverse, to intercept the game and roll with it afoot.

How many of these surging reinforcements were there to cheer Junah? Probably very few. Only the Savannah contingent and a smattering who couldn't resist cheering the underdog.

It was the action.

The battle.

The sense, communicated like quicksilver among the throng, that things were heating up. There was blood in the water.

Junah himself was electrified. Was he seeing the Field? Had he found his Authentic Swing? Yes and yes again. You could see it in his eyes, his stride, in the energy that radiated from him as he strode the fast-drying fairways. Reporters were now pressing closer, pencils scribbling. Cartoon illustrators craned to sketch him.

In the morning round, the galleryites had been a source of terror to Junah. Witnesses to his public mortification, they had only made him want to hide, to recede if he could into invisibility. Now suddenly, now that he was banging the pill, they became his allies. His boosters. His bosom confidants.

As he strode down the fairway, voices rang out. "Get 'em, Junah!" "Knock it stiff!" "Ram it in!" When he struck a drive or an iron, the applause was wild and immediate, followed by yet more fevered shouts of encouragement.

It is something to hear strangers calling your name. Cheering you onward, urging you to triumph. To watch massed formations surge and swell, break into stampedes, jostling one another merely for the chance to glimpse you, to bask in your aurora and, yes (the word is not too strong), worship you.

Junah may have witnessed this before, but he had never experienced it. I of course had done neither. I was astonished at the power, the sheer walloping electricity that surged from the massed galleries. It was palpable. A force as raw and primordial as heat, and all of it focusing like a sun on Junah.

What must he be seeing, beholding the Field? What power and energy were radiating off the auroras of the gallery? Junah ate it up. To be cheered. To be hurrahed and adulated! All fear left his swing. He planted solid and swung from the heels. With each flushed blow, the spectators' cheers rang louder and lustier.

A wild, insane thought began to percolate.

Junah could win.

He could beat Jones and Hagen!

On eight, a 442 par four into the wind, Junah's drive finished within a yard of the spot he had played to in the morning. He had hit a three-iron then into an identical wind. I squinted at the flag and was sure it was a mashie. Two clubs less.

Adrenaline. The jolt of power from the gallery and from Junah's own surging self-confidence. He drilled the mashie stiff. The crowd didn't so much cheer as stand witness in awe. Junah was intoxicated. Invincible. He began to feel there was nothing he couldn't do. To stand at 180, knowing the shot was normally a five-iron, and be able now to go long with a seven . . . all horizons seemed to shoot back to infinity. What couldn't he do?

He began cracking jokes. I heard him tell someone in the gallery, "Bet on me." Vance watched in silence. He could see Junah stealing glances at Jones and Hagen. He had them going. They were tempted to press, to equal his stunning shots that were so electrifying the gallery.

They wouldn't do it of course. Both these champions were far too canny to be drawn into playing an opponent's game. But Junah was making them think. He was making them resist. They were daunted, reaching deep to summon their full powers.

Then there were the women.

Until now the fair element had clustered mostly with Hagen, with minority enthusiasm following Jones. Now I saw a beauty's eyes flirt with Junah, and his eyes smile back. Other belles scooted in like quail, their silk-clad hind ends wriggling as they scurried through a fairway crossing in their covey. Junah didn't gawk but you could see he felt them. At the break of each shot, more maidens rallied into view, flitting before Junah's path on the fairway like eager does seeking the eye of the stud buck.

I felt a terrible chill seeing that. I glanced at Bagger Vance. Before, I had interpreted his silence as his blessing on Junah, like a jockey giving his steed its head. Now I saw a darker light in Vance's eyes.

He was giving Junah rope.

Junah birdied eight, to draw two back of Jones and Hagen. If he could do the same at nine, eminently possible on this downwind par five, he would make the turn in 31.

His three nines would be 41, 35, 31.

He stepped to the tee and absolutely crushed one. A leviathan that snapped the gallery's necks as it streaked from the clubhead, roared mightily into the jet stream and pounded down the slot to finish thirty or forty yards past the three hundred mark.

It was the kind of monster that utterly daunts your opponents. Unmatchable. Hagen and Jones were too smart to try; you could see them simply settle, centering themselves in their own games. They both ripped beauties past 280.

In that surge with the massed gallery down the ninth fairway, Junah seemed almost to levitate. The phrase "walking on air" couldn't be more apt. Members of the gallery, boys and young men, were actually pressing in, just to touch him. All momentum flooded to his side. He had his foes on the run. On the ropes.

Nine was the only hole at Krewe Island that required a carry over water. The shot to the green on this 590-yard par five crossed a small rocky cove, a gorgeous-looking approach to a big green on a bluff. The player going for it in two, as Junah now could after his gorilla drive, was faced with a carry of more than 250 to a wide and deep target that would hold even the hottest, most spinless wood. Jones creased a brassie to the landing area left; Hagen followed with a high cut spoon that rode the wind to the same plateau, about 40 yards short. Now it was Junah's play.

He had driven the ball 330 with a three-club wind at his back: 260 left. I looked; it was a brassie . . . maybe a cloud-riding spoon with the gale pushing from behind with such force. Junah stood beside Bagger Vance, both of them squinting across the cove toward the green rising beyond. The fingers of Junah's hand rested lightly on the knitted head cover. Then they shifted, to the driving iron. Vance shook his head. Junah's hand didn't move; he was so pumped up, he wanted to hit that iron. A 240-yard carry with a hickory-shafted one-iron and a 1931 Spalding Dot. Vance said something I couldn't hear. "I know what I'm feeling," I heard Junah answer. "I can do it."

I had never heard that tone in his voice, at least never to Vance. It was dismissive. Arrogant. Vance pulled his own hand back from the three-wood. I felt a desperate chill. Junah tugged out the driving iron.

There's a kind of sick foreboding that one experiences sometimes at a sporting event. It welled up in me now as I saw the gallery, including the first comely damsel who had wriggled down into Junah's line of sight, thrill at Junah's club selection. He was going over the water with *that*? With an iron? They were already rehearsing the tale to tell their grandchildren. Junah addressed the ball in his perfect easy rhythm. He nailed it. Flush in the sweet spot with all the adrenaline flowing and streaking straight for the flagstick. Vance didn't move, didn't even watch it. The ball started hard and low, like Junah's iron shots always did, then began to climb with the spin as it started to carry the cove. Then the wind hit it. The following wind that Junah was sure would lift it and add that extra bit of juice that the shot needed. But the wind didn't lift it. It knocked it down. Unlike Jones' and Hagen's woods, which had more than enough steam for the carry, Junah's iron needed the spin to climb and the wind wouldn't let the spin take. The ball dropped ten yards short, hit the bluff face before the green and splashed back into the sea.

A groan rose from the gallery. Hagen's eyes flickered once. Vance's hand slid to the bag strap; he hoisted his player's clubs to his shoulder, starting to stride down toward the drop zone at the margin of the cove where Junah would take his one-shot penalty and go at the green with a pitch.

"Where are you going?" Junah's voice was harsh. Vance stopped in his tracks. The gallery froze. What was Junah thinking? The rules allowed him to go forward to the point where the ball crossed the margin of the hazard—in other words 150 yards closer to hole. Why wasn't he going? He wasn't going to hit the shot again—from this same spot?

The gallery had already started forward, overrunning the fairway directly before Junah. Now they realized, *My God, he's going to play from there!* Junah dropped a ball. The marshals were herding the spectators back. Vance said not a word. I looked in Junah's eyes and there was a cold rage, a pride. Vance had become withdrawn, even meek. He didn't scold Junah; he just stepped back and let him hang himself.

As if in the thrall of some demonic spell, Junah took the driving iron again and hit the identical shot. Into the identical sea.

Now the shock wave hit him. You could see his eyes darken. There was disbelief. Then confusion, disorientation. Junah's mind struggled to calculate. How many shots had he thrown away? What was he lying now? How far behind had this madness dropped him? His mind went blank. Refused to make the computations.

"You lie five," Bagger Vance said softly. Junah reeled. Now in his eyes, when he met his caddie's, was not arrogance but humiliation. He was shamed, chastened; he knew what he had done.

And still he had to play.

Still he had to make the death march down to the drop zone at the edge of the cove and somehow play a pitiless downwind pitch over the water that he'd just dumped two balls into and who was to say he wouldn't dump another and another after that?

He got the ball into the hole in eight.

Hagen and Jones both parred.

Junah was now five back of both of them.

He bogeyed ten, pressing off the tee and snap-hooking into a bunker. Blind luck saved him when Hagen and Jones bogeyed too.

"We're trying to come back to you, kid," Hagen wisecracked as they crossed to the eleventh, "but you won't let us."

Junah was dead in the water. You could see it, smell it. It reeked from him. Far worse than his ineptitude in the morning round, which could have been explained as nerves or simply being overmatched.

This was different.

This was a collapse.

This was choking, this was the bottom dropping out, this was the wheels coming off.

A look of empathy played across Jones' face, looking far too much like pity. And all of it was made worse for Junah because he knew it was not that, it was not the pressure or the tension. He had destroyed himself by his own arrogance. With his own hand he had crushed the Grace that had been granted him. Bagger Vance had set the snare that Junah had not just tripped upon, but stampeded into headlong.

Where were the women now?

They had fled. Vanished. Flown. You couldn't even glimpse them in the gallery. . . .

Junah scratched out a wobbly-kneed par on the short eleventh. He barely slopped in a 20-footer for the same on twelve.

We strode down the thirteenth fairway after a miserable pushed fade that left him a full 240 to a desperately tight target. The galleries had evaporated too. All but the ghouls and ambulance chasers.

"Why did you do it?" Junah's voice to Vance was tight with pain. "You set me up!"

"I gave you what you wished for," the caddie answered calmly.

Suddenly Junah's anger surged. "Oh, give it a rest, will you? It's horseshit and I'm tired of listening to it. Who the hell are you to keep serving up this crap? It's a piece of cake to stand on the sidelines holding the bag, to talk and rattle on about . . ."

Junah pulled up, realizing he had overstepped his bounds. "Please, Bagger, forgive me," he blurted. "Don't be angry with me. . . ."

"I am not angry, my friend. Rather, out of my deep love for you, I will answer your question. I will show you who I am."

Junah froze, chastened. "I have failed, Bagger. Here on this field and in all else in my life. I know you've brought me here deliberately, and I know it's out of love for me. Love I can't seem to understand or return. Help me, please. Show me. I am ready at last to see."

T w e n t y - o n e

V ANCE UTTERED NO WORD. He simply motioned to me to take the golf bag from him, which I instantly did. Then he stepped forward, from the caddie side of the bag to the player side. The hair stood up on my neck. Vance was in shirtsleeves, in his caddie cap with his dark eyes veiled in the shadow beneath the brim. Junah stepped back, as if compelled by Vance's force. "Only to you, Junah, will I show myself in all my power. I give you the divine eye with which to see; otherwise the merest fragment of this vision would be your end." The caddie reached to the bag, which I tilted forward for him, presenting the clubs arrayed between their leather dividers; Vance's fingers cradled a single emery-buffed blade; he tugged up Junah's one-iron. Junah turned in the direction of the gallery. How were they reacting to the sight of a caddie suddenly stepping from his servant's role and seizing his player's most dangerous and difficult weapon? I saw Junah's face freeze and then I turned too.

There was no gallery.

Every face, every form had vanished, obscured by the densest, most impenetrable fog I had ever seen. The sky was gone. There was no sun, only a viscous light leaking through the eerie murk from above, and the sound, still present and even more terrifying thereby, of the surf crashing invisibly beyond the mist that enshrouded us. I felt as if we had stepped back ten thousand years, or ten million. A tunnel had formed, excluding all else in the world save we three and the green, 240 yards distant. Even the green had been transformed. There was no flag anymore. Nor had the surface remained its manicured, modern self. It had become raw, a product of nature, yet still recognizably a green; it was whatever the first shepherds or warriors or wanderers saw. Terror struck me, like one feels in the face of Nature unleashing its power, or more precisely, Nature preparing to do so. I glanced to Junah, to see if his eyes were seeing what mine thought they beheld. His expression plunged me deeper into dread; his eyes dark with dismay and disorientation, his soul sensing that this, this thing that was coming, was beyond courage, beyond any response that mortal flesh could produce.

Now Vance, still swiftly, still without a word, dropped three brand-new balata Dots to the turf. The club was in his hands; he stepped to the first ball. Whatever terror had gripped me was now superseded in the hypnotic spell of the sight Junah and I now beheld. Perhaps no one but a golfer, indeed none but a passionate lover of the game, could appreciate the sheer beauty and intelligence—no other words will do—of the way the caddie now placed his hands upon the club.

Motionless, actionless, Vance's grip embodied all motion and all action. His swing, unswung, lay within it. Every aspect of his game and all other games resided silently, pregnantly there, waiting to be brought to form.

Vance coiled and fired.

The shot exploded off the clubface, streaking like a bomb toward the green. Junah gasped. I staggered. The sound was like an artillery shell; the ball thundered through the ether like a midnight freight. Before it had reached the pinnacle of its flight, Vance stepped to the second ball. BOOM! This too detonated skyward, dead flushed; but while the first, still airborne, was drawing toward its target, this its brother arced powerfully from left to right. BOOM! The third ball rocketed away, brushing the grass tops, low and hissing, then screaming as it climbed like a bomber. All three balls were still in the air. "Hardy," Vance spoke in that still, centered voice, "run up and get them. Tell us where they finish."

Somehow I got one foot started, then the other. "Get the balls and return as fast as you can run," Vance called to me. "Don't look back once you've left the green. Wait for nothing, do you hear me?" He didn't have to tell me twice. I took off on a dead run, streaking up the fairway with my heart thundering and my lungs pumping like bellows. One glance backward showed me Vance facing Junah, placing both hands on the champion's shoulders.

Both hands.

Oh Lord, I gulped and kept running. My heart was pounding so wildly, I could see its beating pulse behind both retinas. My eyeballs were flashing. Through shreds of tattered mist I glimpsed fragments of the gallery, frozen like statuary. Vance had made the earth stand in place, or lifted it clean out of the grip of time. Despite my terror, curiosity rose. I wanted to dash off to the side of the fairway, just for a moment, to touch one of the petrified spectators. Were they breathing? Hard as stone? I was at the green now. There was no flag, as I said; the turf was not machine mown but tight packed, dense and perfect as the surface of a stone worn smooth by aeons. It was the most impeccable green I had ever seen, shaped only by Nature. There was the hole, flagless, etched precisely to four and one-quarter inches.

In it were the three Spaldings.

I snatched them and turned back, Vance's words blazing in my brain. *Don't look back, wait for nothing.* But of course I did. I couldn't help squinting back down the fairway, past my heaving lungs, through my strobing eyeballs. Junah now knelt before Vance in a posture of abject terror. He was seeing something. Being shown something. I saw his arms raised involuntarily in a gesture of fear and self-protection. I couldn't go back there. I would die if I did. I turned back toward the green. Where could I run? What direction could I flee in? The sight of the gallery, massed behind the green in its stony paralysis, only redoubled my terror.

I had done what Vance told me not to. I had looked back. Instantly the earth began to tremble. The green shuddered; the turf beneath my feet cracked, black gaps spidering two inches wide, four, six . . . "God help me!" I cried and turned, with all my ten-year-old's speed, to race back down toward Junah and Vance. It was too late. The fairway was quaking beneath me. The skies went black; a storm that had apparently been building beyond the fog now broke with all its massed fury. The heavens split overhead. Wind and gale-blasted rain struck down in a deluge; I was knocked off my feet by the first sidelong blast, I fell, clawing at the fairway grass, which was now lying over flat on its side in the gale. How can I describe the sound? The wind began as a low, eerie, almost musical moan, like ten thousand boys blowing across the mouths of ten thousand pop bottles; then it rose to a cry, a wail, a scream; beyond that it ceased to be a sound and became a force, something physical and palpable that shuddered you in your very cells, vibrating with such power and intensity that nothing could withstand it. Your heart struggled to beat but couldn't, the sound absorbed the tissue, the muscle, the blood itself in the shriek of its vibration. It consumed your essence, deafening, monstrous, cataclysmic. I was blown backward, tumbling across the fairway, which continued to shudder from beneath, assaulted simultaneously from the planet's core and from the heavens. I heard voices, skyborne and titanic, and when I looked, the field had been transformed.

It was the battle.

The battle of twenty-one thousand years ago.

That turf which had been fairway a moment past was now torn and sundered by the hoof-strikes of warhorses, the tread of armored infantry digging for traction, the pounding wheels and axles of monstrous engines of war. Rain and blood mingled in the chewed-up muck as steel-girded phalanxes surged past and the clamor of shield upon shield thundered heavenward into the storm.

I saw Junah, valorous as a god, not his present self but some brilliant primordial incarnation, slashing forward aboard a war chariot.

I saw myself, not the boy I was now but a man grown, breast to breast with the foe amid the thunder of the battle line.

I saw others, yet unborn in this century, and knew them as my comrades across eternity.

A sound like the spine of the earth itself cracking split the banshee howl of the storm. It was the fifteenth and sixteenth holes, the land itself calving into the sea.

In my wild tumble I blew into a fairway bunker.

It was the Scottish kind, as all of Krewe Island's were, with bricks of turf stacked along the leeward wall. These I now dug my fingernails into and clung to for dear life. The gale howled. Sand blasted from the bunker, the pit itself was scoured clean in seconds. I buried my cheek against the turf bricks, praying with every terrified fiber of my being as the bricks blew away, first in ones and twos, then in clusters.

Somehow I knew that this was not just the battle, but the Great Atlantic Storm, the storm of '38, seven years in the future, the blow that would efface Krewe Island, all of it save the eighteenth hole. And I knew more. That storm and battle had happened before, millennia past, in another age like ours on the brink of apocalypse. I squeezed my eyes as tightly shut as I could, but still I could see:

That horrible tower I had glimpsed in Junah's book, the illustration of the limbs and mouths. Now the world opened, the continents cracked. It was all Vance. Vance in some horrific cosmic form rending the earth as if it were a bauble. The planet was merely an atom to him. Less than an atom. In the maws of his countless mouths, the warriors in all their valor fell and perished.

I was next. I felt the fragile flame of my life being blown out like a candle in the gale. The bunker blew apart; the full force of the storm struck me, I began to tumble again, blown wildly. Then a hand seized mine. I couldn't open my eyes, the windblast was too overwhelming. It was Junah. Junah in the present. "Hang on!" he cried in the gale's teeth. "Hang on, Hardy!"

Up he drew me; I clung blindly as his strong arm lifted me and there, on the one piece of the thirteenth hole still standing, collapsed gasping beside Junah and Bagger Vance.

"Ran!" I cried Junah's first name. "Are you all right?!"

"Shh, Hardy." Junah held me with all his athlete's strength. The gale yet shrieked. Junah stood in a posture of reverence, bowing his head before Vance in fear and awe.

"Junah is unharmed," Vance spoke and laid his hand gently on the champion's shoulder. Now the fire, the flame of destruction in Vance's eye softened, relented and became love, the sweetest, most heartbreaking affection, pure and rapt and unconditional. I began to weep, I was so frightened and confused.

"It's okay, Hardy." Junah held me comfortingly. "We're alive. It's still the earth beneath us."

"Why did you disobey me?" Vance addressed me sternly. "You were not supposed to see this. A fraction of a glimpse could have killed you with its power!"

The merest gesture of his hand . . . and the storm stilled. Fog still enshrouded us; we remained enwrapped in the tunnel, the gallery absent and invisible. But the heavens stood again intact and, most merciful of all, that horrible keening wind withdrew to silence.

"Let me get a look at you," Vance spoke, now with kindness, bending toward me. His warm hands settled on my shoulders; I felt myself recomposing, coming together again into something that felt mercifully like myself.

"Who are you?" I heard my voice beg of Vance; then to Junah: "Who is he, Ran? You know, don't you? But you won't tell me!" I turned again to Vance. "Am I alive? Are we dead? Are you going to kill us?"

"Did you find the three balls?" Vance asked quietly.

"Yes!" I shouted, furious with fear and frustration.

"And where were they?"

"You know damn well where they were! Who *are* you? How do you make this stuff happen?"

Junah held me firmly. "It's over, Hardy. Calm down."

"I'll calm down when he tells me who he is!"

Vance only held out his hand for the balls. I clung to Junah. "Tell him, Bagger," the champion spoke softly. Then, trembling himself: "I need to hear your words as well, to quench the fear and confusion in my heart."

Vance's gaze regarded Junah with pure, limitless love. Then he too knelt, turning my face from where it was, buried in the cotton of Junah's shirt, to face him. He took the three balls from my fist and spoke softly, directly to me.

"I come again in every age, taking on human form to perform the duty I set myself. I return to right the balance of things."

These cryptic words only made me more terrified. "Return from where? What do you mean, 'human form'?" I twisted to Junah for help, but the champion only held me more firmly, turning me back toward Vance as if to say, *Be patient, listen.*

Vance knelt on the grass before me, lowering his eyes to the same level as mine. I peered into them. They were bottomless, endless, without boundary or limit. Up close I could smell again that pungent, wild, suprahuman odor.

"You will know me in every age by the way deluded men respond to me. They despise me, as you yourself did when we first met in the slave kitchen."

"That's not true! I just . . ."

I pulled up, tripped by guilt and truth. Bagger Vance spoke again, his voice even softer and more still.

"Before Time was, I am. Before Form was, I am."

The hair stood straight up on my forearms. My mouth went dry, I began to tremble. . . .

"I am the Field *and* the Knower," Bagger Vance said. "Everything that is, is brought into being and sustained by me."

He glanced once to the battlefield and immediately the sundered turf rose intact from the fog. Spectators reanimated, fairways resumed their wonted contour, the late sun shone brilliantly through. There was Jones, stepping forth in midstride as if nothing had happened. Hagen continued a joke he had been telling. Everything revivified exactly as it had been, as if but a thousandth of a second, a thousandth of a thousandth, had elapsed. Vance rose and resumed his position behind the bag, on the caddie side.

I stood tight beside Junah, with my arm around him and his around me. "How will I ever hit the ball now?" Junah asked Bagger Vance. "How can I even move after what you've just shown us?"

For a moment Vance did not answer. Instead he held out the three Spalding Dots. One he handed to me, one to Junah, and one he kept himself. Then he spoke, addressing the champion. "I have schooled you throughout this day in the hidden ways and mysteries of golf. Now listen, Junah, to the seminal unspoken core. The final and supreme secret of the Supreme Game."

The reanimated galleries had by now turned again to Junah, in the exact attitude they had held before. In their eyes was the expectation of his continued self-immolation, which expectation was reinforced by the ashen, deeply shaken state in which Junah now resided. The galleries waited, pitiless as wolves. Waited to watch him continue to fall apart.

"Loneliness." Vance spoke the single word. "This is the scythe of the game, its midnight heart and terror. The utter, excruciating isolation which attacks the player under pressure such as you have struggled with today. Listen to me, Junah, while I deliver to you the supreme and ultimate secret of the game."

Junah turned to Vance with every fiber of his attention. I stood like granite, transfixed.

"Forget all else, Junah, but remember this: *You are never alone.* You have your caddie. You have me.

"More devoted than a mother, more faithful than a lover, I

stand by your side always. I will never abandon you. No sin, no lapse, no crime however heinous can make me desert you, nor yield up to you any less than my ultimate fidelity and love.

> *"Who walks his path beside me*
> *Feels my hand upon him always.*
> *No effort he makes is wasted,*
> *Nor unseen, unguided by me.*

"Therefore, Junah, rest in me. Enter the Field like a warrior. Purged of ego, firm in discipline, seeking no reward save the stroke itself. Give the shot to me. I am your Self, the Ground of your being, your Authentic Swing."

Vance finished, as softly as he had begun, then tilted the bag, proffering it and its weapons before the champion.

"Now strike, my friend, as I have taught you. Hold nothing back."

Twenty-two

IN THE DOZENS OF ACCOUNTS that appeared in the press the following day this next stroke, the one-iron that Junah holed out for an eagle, was cited variously as the "Lazarus shot," "the Governor's reprieve," a "miracle," a "bolt from the ether." It was described as "Promethean," "Euclidian" and "plucked from that place where the sun don't shine." Grantland Rice quoted the old Georgia saw:

> Even a blind squirrel finds an acorn every once in a while.

They spoke of it as raw luck rescuing a man dangling by his fingertips, a fortuitous thunderbolt that had breathed fresh fire into Junah's lifeless form. There were comments on Junah's reaction to the shot. How, despite the galleries going berserk around the green as the ball lit, spun left and curled down the slope into the cup, Junah had remained impassive, unruffled. They marveled that he hadn't exhibited more emotion or elation. That all he'd done was meet his caddie's eyes as if to acknowledge his contribution in club selection; then hand the weapon back and stride, deeply and profoundly concentrated, toward the green.

You may imagine the state of mind I was in at this point. Looking back, I credit the resiliency of youth, a boy's sheer capacity for imagination, with preserving my sanity. In an odd way, I had even somewhat taken it all in stride. I felt the relief at least that Vance would not repeat any of this cosmic drama. What more could he do, after stopping time, freezing the globe, destroying and restoring the planet? My feelings about being near him oscillated between love and terror. I was still half-petrified when he fell into step beside me, striding toward the thirteenth green. "What I said to Junah back there," he began when I said nothing but kept striding uncertainly forward, "was for your ears too, Hardy. You too are never alone, nor ever will be. Those who seek lesser teachers go unto them. My players come always to me."

Will it make sense, Michael and Irene, if I tell you how much the phrase "my players" meant to me? I was so proud, and so relieved, that Vance considered me one of "his players." All fear left me instantly.

"Remember when you saw those gulls in the storm," Vance asked me, "and you had the sense of them 'playing'?" How could he know that? I didn't even question it anymore. "Your instincts were astute," he said. "Play is the activity most pleasing to me. Can you guess why?"

Of course I couldn't.

"Because it is authentic."

But now his voice lowered, became more private.

"Listen to me, young Hardy. A day will come for you when play becomes torment. When you will be drowning, not in water but on dry land. In that hour remember me. I will preserve you."

With that, he placed his hand on my pocket, the pocket where I had tucked my Spalding Dot.

I still have that ball.

In fact I have brought it with me tonight.

But let me return to Junah.

He had pulled to within three of Jones and Hagen. Five holes now remained.

Let me describe them in detail, this final handful, and, I hope, the emotion that accompanied them. For by now the spectators and the players had been caught up completely in the roller coaster of the afternoon round.

Junah's eagle had electrified the gallery, which was now swelling by twos and fives and scores. The sun meanwhile had traversed far more of its course than the officials had anticipated; it was dropping with perhaps an hour, an hour and a half at most until it would vanish over the wetlands and close the match out in the dark.

There was no time to dawdle.

Junah, Jones and Hagen all nailed solid mid-irons to the par-three fourteenth and found their balls stacked one behind the other on the identical line to the cup—Jones eighteen feet out, Hagen inside him by a foot and Junah six inches closer. There was a bit of uneasy jostling as each repaired his ball mark, Hagen and Junah positioning their dimes at right angles to the side, one and two putter-heads out, being almost comically overcareful not to tread in each other's or Jones' line. Time was passing. Daylight wasting. "Hell," the Haig cracked, "let's be men and play stymies." I think Jones would have risked it, master of that shot that he was, had the contest's medal-play setup not precluded it.

Bobby lined up his putt and stroked it. It curled off, a whisker on the low side. Hagen, overcompensating perhaps from the roll he had just seen, rapped his a fraction too hard; it scooted past on the high side. Junah stepped up, still glowing from his eagle, and split the difference. The ball dove straight into the heart.

Something marvelous began to happen.

All conversation ceased among the players. A dialogue of wit and brilliance began to be played out in their shots. Junah was deep in the Field. The gallery knew. Hagen knew. Jones knew. On fifteen when Junah, swinging it seemed utterly without effort, bombed a drive beyond any of the monsters he had yet launched, the sense solidified among all watching that this man would not crumble any further. He was rolling. That was it. No one would get off the hook.

Jones and Hagen rose to it. It has been said of both that, when called for, they could crank their swings open another notch and add twenty or thirty yards. This they now did. Jones driving off the par-five fifteenth seemed to move through the ball in slow motion. The shot rocketed skyward as if it would never come down. Hagen followed with an attempted home run that turned over, caught the wrong side of a fairway bunker and careened wildly into jungle grass. Tawdry Jones raced after it, planting his flag in cabbage up to the knees of his plus fours. When we got to the ball, it was sitting up like a plover's egg on the single tuft of marsh grass in a radius of a dozen feet. It couldn't have been more impeccably teed if Sir Walter's own valet had done it. Hagen slashed a driver out of the muck that flew and bounded all the way to a greenside bunker, 260 away. The gallery surged to the green in joyous hysteria, just shy of out-and-out bedlam.

Here Jones and Junah, both on in two, faced probably the most impossible putts I have ever seen. Let me attempt a picture of them. Jones was outside, about fifty feet away; Junah perhaps three feet closer. Both balls sat on the upper tier of a two-level green, with the flag on the lower and a dizzyingly slick slope in between. The putt ran fiercely downgrain all the way, and worse, it was dry. The elevated green had drained exceptionally well and been dewatered even further by the hard coastal wind. It was greased lightning. To stop the ball anywhere near the hole, the putt had to be ghosted to the absolute edge of the slope top, so that it was barely creeping when it started over. And, if these difficulties weren't enough, the slope also bore a wicked right-to-left break following the grain.

Jones looked it over from all four quadrants. This was ample testament to the dauntingness of the shot, as Jones invariably stepped to his putts briskly and without over-rumination. It was riveting to watch his face now, deep in concentration, oblivious of the gallery, of his opponents, of everything except the slope, the grain and the ball. His eyes blinked as he thought; he absently chewed his lip pacing back to behind the ball. He was sensing the green through his spikes, through his soles. I was directly behind his ball and the downgrain was shining like a wet slicker. He was ready. He set Calamity Jane before the ball as he always did, checked the line once, then lifted the putter blade and set it behind the ball; another glance to the cup and then he stroked it.

The ball crept forward toward the top of the ski jump. I was sure he had mishit it, even scuffed it, it was going so slowly. It would stop five feet short of the downslope for sure. But Jones had not moved. There was no indication in his posture that he had erred; he was frozen, watching the ball inch forward exactly as he had intended. By God, he was right! The ball kept crawling and creeping . . . to the very brink of the downslope, hovering, almost stopping, it seemed it actually *did* stop, still twenty-five feet above the hole, and then, with an infinitesimal move, it nudged clear of the last blade of grass and the downslope caught it. Here it came. Slow at first, then faster, faster, picking up speed and breaking down that wicked slippery grain, burning the edge of the cup and sliding remorselessly onward, six feet by, eight feet, ten, and still creeping resistlessly onward till it finally wobbled to a stop twelve feet past.

The gallery groaned and then applauded. A better putt could not have been stroked. A thousand further tries would produce nothing superior. The putt was just damn impossible!

Now the spectators turned and watched Junah study it. Here, theoretically at least, was an opening. If Jones could not get his twelve-footer in, he would par, not birdie. If Junah could somehow get this putt down in two, he would pick up a shot. But how could he, or anyone including Harry Houdini, stop the ball near the hole on that ice-slick downhill?

Junah took his sand iron. The gallery oohhed in surprise and puzzlement. The man was on the green; what in the world was he doing with a wedge? I saw Hagen nod and chuckle. Junah stepped to the ball, then turned, facing not at the hole but at 90 degrees, more, 110 degrees. He was going to chip it *off* the green, up the slope at right angles to the hole, and let it drift down across the grain instead of down. Jones turned to Keeler with a crooked grin. He had thought of this too, it was clear, but judged it too risky. Junah settled over the shot. Checked the line once, twice. There was no way to plot this by azimuth; it was all feel and instinct.

He swung.

A crisp little half-chip that nipped the ball, scuffing the perfect grass of the green, taking a divot the size of a tablespoon, and lofted the spinning sphere up off the green onto the steep sloping collar above. For a second terror struck me; I was sure he had hit it too hard. Then I realized, he intended this! Junah wasn't coming in from the side, but from the rear!

The ball struck the upper bank five or six feet past the collar, kicked laterally another three, then began trickling rearward, losing some of its speed as it bobbled through the taller grass of the fringe, then dribbled out onto the green forty feet above the hole and directly behind it. Down it came. Slowly at first, then picking up speed, down, down on the much less severe slope from the rear . . . incredibly, on line, but still gathering pace just as Jones' ball had. Oh no. Would it rocket past? Would it squirt by like his? Here it came, missing the cup by half an inch and scooting beyond, in the opposite direction. Two feet . . . four . . . six! But wait, it was on the same grain that had confounded Jones' putt. Only Junah's ball was going up, not down. Against the grain, not with it. The grass grabbed it like a mountain brake on a truck. The ball slowed, trembled, stopped; then started in reverse! Drifting, crawling, creeping, with infinite slowness, half a turn at a time it meandered back down, down, finally ghosting to a stop a foot and a half below the hole.

It was one of those shots whose brilliance evokes not cheers, but laughter. Tension-release laughter. The galleryites whistled and shook their heads and just howled.

Birdie for Junah. Pars for Hagen and Jones. Junah was now one shot back.

"Someone wake this kid up," Hagen joked as they climbed the rise to the sixteenth tee. Junah never heard, so deep was his concentration, though Hagen said it for him and to him from only an arm's length away.

Now fresh spectators were arriving in half dozens and dozens. The press too, smelling the story. Daylight was failing; already on the tee the chief marshals were dispatching their minions two holes ahead, circling cars around the eighteenth green so the headlights could illuminate it.

Let me describe a shot Jones played on sixteen as it, like Junah's driver on six, was one of the half-dozen most courageous I have ever seen.

It was a three-foot putt.

Sixteen was a short par four, 360 off the tee we played in the morning but now only 310 with the afternoon markers pushed all the way forward. The wind had shifted to quartering from behind; the green was reachable, though spooky with the light failing and a ring of lethal bunkers protecting all approaches save one lane no more than 15 feet wide. Junah and Hagen both played prudent one-irons, leaving themselves in the fairway 80 or 90 yards out. Jones went to Jeannie Deans, his driver. What was he thinking? Possibly he was aiming deliberately for the greenside bunkers, figuring he had as good a chance of getting down in two from there as from the fairway, and without fear of dumping a pitch into the sand from 90 yards out. Whatever his strategy, it succeeded brilliantly. He unleashed a bomb off the tee, dead on line all the way, striking the 15-foot gap smack in the center and scooting nimbly onto the green, curling to a stop inside the shadow of the flag.

This was not one of those shots whose effect is appreciated only on later reflection. Hagen and Junah felt the full impact right now. This was Jones declaring for all that he was the Man, invincible, waiting only till the ninth inning to pack his opponents away. Fun and games were over. Bobby was taking charge.

Hagen and Junah rained valiant pitches in to ten and twelve feet respectively. Junah made and Hagen missed. The gallery seemed to press in, if it were possible, even more tightly around the green. Jones stepped to the uphill six-footer for his eagle. Against Hagen's par, Bobby would pick up two here. Even

Junah's birdie would do him no more service than to cut his loss to a single stroke. The gallery had it figured; Keeler had it figured; without doubt Bobby did too.

Jones missed.

Maybe spooked by the quickness of his putt on the previous hole, he misjudged this one. Left it a foot short. The gallery groaned. Still it was no problem; Jones would tap in for his birdie and stride to seventeen no worse than when he began the hole.

He missed the tap-in.

Didn't just miss, but rammed it three and a half feet past!

Now he was staring down the gut of a left-to-right downhill slider not for an eagle or a birdie but a par, a par that would after all his heroics *lose* him a stroke, to Junah anyway, and yawning like the maw of doom before him was the very real possibility that he would miss this too! Would he four-putt? Would this go on all day? Would his ball keep scooting back and forth past this hole interminably? The gallery's golfing terrors intuited all this; you could see them holding their breath, averting their eyes as the debacle loomed in the failing light.

Jones stepped up and made his par.

The mob went berserk. Jones had his four. So did Hagen. Junah had three. They strode to seventeen all tied!

Now the gallery truly threatened to get out of hand. It got a little scary with the pushing and shoving; the marshals and a number of Georgia State Patrolmen had to close in tight around the players; I held on to Bagger Vance's hand for all I was worth. The spectators surged and jostled; there was barely enough room on the tee to swing. Jones wanted to tee his ball off the left marker and couldn't, the gallery could not be moved back; those in the rear were pressing in so hard that their fellows in front, however willing they may have been to oblige the champion, simply could not move back.

Now came the next excruciating, heartbreaking shot.

Let me describe the hole.

I would rank it, the seventeenth at Krewe Island, with Pebble Beach's eighteenth, the thirteenth at Pine Valley and the fourteenth, "Foxy," at Royal Dornoch. One of the handful of greatest holes in the world.

Par four, 444 that played like 490. The wind was against, freshening now, coming from the south along Barnsall Point at about two clubs. The green, which you had to squint at in the gathering darkness, as your eyes teared slightly from the salt breeze in your face, was elevated about forty feet along a sand bluffline (add two more clubs for the carry) and offset about thirty yards to the right from the line of the fairway. The drive was to a broad, scooped-out landing area that kicked in from both right and left, effectively funneling the shot into a steadily rising uphill that sloped gently left, thus carrying the ball, the longer it was hit, farther left and away from the green. There were four pot bunkers left and five grass mounds right. A big drive down the right against the kick of the fairway left the player a heartstoppingly long iron that had to carry a wide ravine and a sheer bluff face to reach the elevated green. The surface would hold, that wasn't the problem. It was the awesome carry, the precarious target and more dangerous still the wind, the relentless shear that rose from behind the green and would knock off line everything but the most perfectly struck shot and send it tumbling right or left downhill to extremely daunting approach areas that were not bunkered, making them even more difficult because the player couldn't count on any backstop from the sand, or generate any spin or loft with an explosion shot.

The alternative strategy was to follow the line of the fairway and play left off the tee. This lessened somewhat the difficulty of the approach because of a grass ridge backstopping the green on the flank, but left the player thirty or forty yards farther from the green, into spoon or even brassie country, and all with that excruciating long wind-buffeted carry.

Down the right, the hole was a killer par four; down the left, a legitimate five.

The rowdy gallery was calling out Junah's name as he stepped to the tee off his run of five under in the last four holes. He himself was deep in the Field. He was meeting no one's eyes and speaking to no one save Bagger Vance. You could see how relaxed he was, yet how utterly focused. Shots were talking to him. He was listening. Gone completely was any sense of being daunted by the two great champions he was facing. Junah felt every bit their equal, not tomorrow maybe, not the day after, but today, now. On this day he was their match and, by God, he intended to carry it to them.

They knew it. There were no more jokes. No more wisecracks. This was deadly business.

Junah teed it right. He wasn't taking either of the strategies Mackenzie had intended in the design. He was going farther right, aiming deliberately for a patch of lightish rough, to the right of the five grass mounds and in a direct line to the green. It was the boldest shot possible. If he pulled it off, if luck held with a decent lie, a big drive would leave a mid-iron in, instead of a driving iron or even a four-wood. More to the point, the duneline protected the shot somewhat from the wind; since the green held, this would make the approach considerably easier. Junah was gambling. A birdie here would gain one shot for sure and maybe two.

It could win the match.

He fired.

Another cannon shot that snapped the spectators' necks as it boomed off the clubface, rose and soared precisely where Junah had aimed it. "Hop . . . hop," I heard my voice rooting as it streaked down for the rough. It did! One solid skip, another short jump and it rolled to a stop. We could see it! The white of the ball just peeking from the longish grass . . . The lie was playable; Junah's gamble had, so far at least, paid off.

This was the first and only time in the match that I saw Hagen react with real, as opposed to gamesman's, emotion. He was furious. This was too much, that an amateur of Trans-Miss capabilities should continue to pull off these ridiculously valiant and damn near impossible shots. The Haig had had enough. He teed his ball low and went after it, on the same line Junah had taken. It can be truly said of Hagen that, even at his most fearsome, there was always a touch of wit or irony to his play. His opponents, even as he crushed them, were always left with the sense that they had been outplayed or outthought rather than overpowered. Suddenly that changed. The Haig ripped that drive from the soles of his shoes; like Junah's it boomed down the channel-way, hit even harder. The gallery gasped. The shot held Junah's line, longer even, but at the very last it drew just ten feet farther left, caught a left-kicking mound and tailed down off the slope in the rough to finish impeccably in the fairway, and every bit as long as Junah's.

Jones followed with a drive that was merely spectacular. Two-seventy down the left, onto a level lie on the short grass. Still he too had a daunting one-iron or four-wood into that wind-whipped uphill target.

The gallery surged around the competitors as they strode off the tee. It was getting dark, storm clouds were lowering. Officials had sent runners ahead to pull automobiles around the landing area as well as greenside on the eighteenth. If the clouds lowered further or play was delayed for any reason, their headlights would be needed just so the players could see what they were aiming for off the tee. Would we even get in in time? The competitors lengthened their strides, glancing at the fast-sinking sun. It was unthinkable that the match would be called on account of darkness with but a single hole left to play.

I stuck tight beside Junah all the way up the seventeenth. I had been separated once in the mob rush and didn't want it again. Let me describe Junah's state if I can. Unswayed by the rush and surge all around him, he strode with utter composure as if tuned to an internal metronome. His very stride seemed fixed on a rhythm heard only in his own head. He was immersed in the Field, seeking that dimension beyond our three and perhaps even beyond four. I could sense, and so could the galleries, who were electrified by the prospect, that Junah thought he would win. Knew he could win. He never overtly glanced to Bagger Vance or met the caddie's eye, yet every cell seemed to be tuned intuitively to him. Like Ajax or Achilles sensing that a god is fighting beside him, he veritably glowed with courage and confidence. Yet it was held absolutely in check with a light but relentless discipline. He was a warrior. Purged of ego, disciplined, focused, without fear or hope, living with every fiber of his essence in the present and only the present.

Hagen and Jones drew the bulk of the gallery with them down onto the wide flat where their balls had come to rest. Junah's shot from the high slope would have to carry a ravine of about forty feet, then the sheer fifty-foot bluff face that fronted the green. This and the slickness of the slope discouraged most of the spectators, who didn't want to be trapped out there on the promontory while their fellows surged ahead and got all the best spots around the green and along the eighteenth. When we reached Junah's ball there was only Junah, Bagger Vance, me and several marshals, with the massed thousands surging just below in the lighter rough and down across the fairway surrounding Jones and Hagen. The lie was fine, not too high and not too tight; you could spin it. Junah never blinked, just assessed it coldly, remaining deep in his detached rhythm. He squinted up toward the green. The pin was visible, closer than we had dreamed of and shining in a shaft of late sunlight that pierced the clouds like an omen. "I was thinking mid," I heard him say to Vance, meaning a five-iron, "but now it looks like less."

"Hit the mid-iron," Vance said and Junah accepted this assessment instantly. He plucked the club from the bag.

Below on the fairway, Jones set up and rifled a one-iron that lacked no more than three feet of reaching the upper level and finishing stiff. Instead it caught the last arc of upslope and spun away left and down, coming to rest thirty-five feet away and on the lower level. A brilliant shot, masterful under these gusty darkening conditions. But not a birdie. Not a likely one anyway.

Now Hagen played. A mid-iron, the same club Junah held but, from his lie down the hill, the equivalent of twenty yards farther out. The Haig killed it. The shot bore like a bullet through the wind and tore into the green, dead on line and one flag-length short. It took a single hop, when its spin would have kicked in and stopped it dead, but . . . it hit the pin! The ball caromed off, all backspin gone, and skittered sideways onto the apron right. You could hear Hagen's teeth grind from forty yards away. The gallery groaned and then cheered. The Haig was okay, twenty-five feet from the stick, but he too was out of realistic birdie range.

This was luck and Junah knew it. The gallery knew it. Fate was with him, they all sensed. Even Hagen, cursing as he pulled up below to watch Junah's shot, may have felt that this wasn't his day and wasn't Bobby's.

Junah was ready. He stood behind the ball as he always did, checking the line one last time as he settled the club into his grip, letting the shaft find its nestle beneath the heel of the left hand, then rocking the thumb down and closing the pad of the right palm impeccably above it. He let the two middle fingers of his right hand find their place around the leather, then the little finger curled over, crooking into place to ride atop the first knuckle of the left hand. There was a loose stalk of grass blowing about two feet behind Junah's ball; with his clubhead he nonchalantly flicked it, it blew away in the wind. Junah took a step toward the ball. He glanced once toward the target to recheck his line and then . . .

The ball moved!

An inch. No more. Just slid off its grassy perch and settled an inch to the side.

My heart froze in terror.

Oh my God! In what was surely no more than a thousandth of a second, every internal process in my body went into slow motion.

It was clear instantly that this was disaster. A one-stroke penalty. Instead of firing at the green in two with a chance to upend his opponents and seize the match's momentum, Junah would now be shooting three, hoping to hang on to a bogey and, on this most dangerous and difficult of holes, possibly worse. More bitter still was the psychological dislocation. How could Junah refind his focus? There were no holes left to regroup on.

All this raced through my brain in a tenth of a second.

In another tenth I grasped at this straw: that somehow I hadn't seen right. Maybe the ball hadn't moved. It was an optical illusion! A speck in my wind-blurred eye. But one look at Junah's face dispelled that fantasy.

He knew the rule as well as I. As well as every golfer. A player may remove without penalty a loose impediment lying within a club-length of the ball, but

if the ball move after any such loose impediment has been touched by the player . . . the player shall be deemed to have caused the ball to move and *the penalty shall be one stroke*.

It counted for nothing that Junah hadn't touched the ball, that his actions had not been the cause of its moving. All that mattered was that it had moved.

How could this happen? It wasn't fair!

Then, still in the first two tenths of a second, my brain seized upon a terrible alternative. No one had seen the ball move. Not even Bagger Vance, who was ten feet down the hill. Just Junah and I. In the three-inch grass no one else could see it. No one would know.

We could lie!

Pretend nothing happened.

Just hit the ball. Say nothing.

This thought flashed like an evil comet across my brain. Was Junah thinking it too? Could we pull it off? I raised my eyes to see the expression on his face. . . .

But he was already turning away toward the fairway, with the club lowering in his left hand and his right arm raised in the direction of Jones, Hagen and the officials. "Bob! Haig!" Junah's voice rose clear and firm above the wind. "I have to call a shot on myself."

Both of them blinked, shock on their faces. Junah came several more steps down the slope. "The ball moved."

A chill coursed through the gallery as word spread and they realized what had happened. Those who were non-golfers or new to the game reacted with disbelief and outrage at what they perceived to be the injustice of the penalty. It seemed so unfair that the match, which had been fought so long and so valorously, should turn on such a trivial mischance. You mean the ball moves one inch, by accident, to a place no better than it was before—and the man loses the match because of it! If lightning had slain one of their fellows right there among them, the gallery could not have been more staggered. Not just for the penalty stroke, but for the trauma, the psychological shock. Players collapse. The air rushes from their balloon. I saw a man in the gallery fighting tears. Others were ashen-faced. Hagen, Jones, the marshals and scorers had come up the slope and were now gathered in various glum postures around the ball. No one wanted the penalty assessed; their questions all sought the same salvation: could Junah be mistaken, was it possible that the ball had *not* moved, that he had not displaced the loose impediment?

Dougal McDermott read aloud from the Rules. " '. . . a ball is deemed to "move" if it leave its original position in the least degree; but . . . not . . . if it merely oscillate and come to rest in its original position.' Is she diff'rent? Can ye be sartain? Sometimes a ball will shudder, then settle back."

Junah shook his head. "It was there. It rolled to here."

Hagen stood now at Junah's shoulder. "Hit it quick, kid, before you have time to think about it." He strode away, gallantly, wanting to clear the arena for his opponent, let him have his room, his air to breathe. I saw Jones catch Junah's eye just for an instant, a flicker so brief you would have missed it if you'd glanced away even for a second. It was a look that had nothing to do with trophies or triumphs, that would have been as apt for a two-dollar Nassau as for the claret jug of the British Open. A simple acknowledgment, man to man, of an action honorably taken. My glance turned to Bagger Vance, whose eyes were lit as well. He moved beside Junah and spoke, almost too softly to hear.

"In this hour," he said, "you have reached me."

In the press the next day there were numerous mentions of the tears in Junah's eyes at this moment, and the way he and his caddie embraced briefly with emotion. Reporters chalked it up to self-pity, shock, the pain or disappointment of the moment. None of course could have guessed the truth.

As Vance released Junah from their embrace, his own eyes were moist with an emotion bottomless and paternal. I saw him stride quickly to McDermott and the marshals; he began speaking with them privately, seeming to indicate that he was experiencing stomach cramps. My father, Judge Anderson and the elders reacted with alarm.

What was this?

Vance was walking off!

There was a surge of the town fathers, a brief muddled confrontation; I couldn't hear what was said but clearly saw Judge Anderson clutching Vance's arm, pleading with him, eyes wide with concern; *don't go, don't go,* you could read the Judge's lips. Vance was firm; he detached himself with resolve. The marshals indicated it was official; I could see them communicating the news to Jones, Hagen and their caddies and see them acknowledge and accept it. What would happen now? Who would take Junah's bag?

Vance had turned back now and crossed to Junah. "Remember, I am ever with you," he said in his calm, centered voice. Then he took off his caddie's cap and motioned to me. In near-panic I scurried to his side, already knowing what was coming and shaking with dread at the terrible responsibility. There was Junah's bag. Vance slipped it from his shoulder and set it upright on the turf before me, strap extended toward my trembling hand.

"The man is yours, Hardy," he said. "Take him in."

Twenty-three

I N AN INSTANT Vance had vanished, stepping into the gallery, which parted in surprise and shock before him, then closed, swallowing him. He was gone! What would I do now? A dozen potential catastrophes flashed before my eyes. What if I clubbed Junah wrong, here or, worse, on eighteen? What if his shot to the green went short or long because of me? What if my fear threw him off, what if my anxiety was communicated to him? What if I choked; what if I stepped in Jones' or Hagen's line; what if, fighting through the gallery, I burst forth too suddenly and accidentally kicked Junah's ball? And these were only my selfish fears. I imagined myself in Junah's place. How must he feel, facing the shot of his life in the match of his life, suddenly bereft of his guide and mentor, thrust instead into the care of a terrified ten-year-old? I considered with utmost seriousness dropping the bag and fleeing, or crying aloud to the gallery for someone more experienced, anyone more worthy than I. Should

I race after Vance? Chase him down through the crowd and beg him to return? Yet already I knew, as I'm sure did Junah, that Vance had vanished not merely in the figurative sense. He was gone. We would never see him again. At least not as he had been, for us and with us.

With this realization a terrible gravity settled upon my young boy's shoulders. I grew five years in that instant. I felt words forming inside me and knew they were his, they were Vance's. I stepped forward and spoke directly to Junah. "The Rules require you to replace the ball. Back where it was, before it rolled. Otherwise it's another stroke penalty."

Junah blinked. His eyes met mine. "Thank you, Hardy. You're absolutely right."

In the emotion and confusion everyone, even Jones and Hagen, had forgotten this vital footnote to the rule. Surely someone would have caught it before Junah hit; a marshal or official, or Jones or Hagen themselves, would have recalled and stopped Junah before he played. But it was I who in fact spoke. In an instant I felt calm and centered. I knew Vance was with me as he was with Junah; I had only to open my mouth and his words would come out.

Junah replaced the ball. The gallery had by now swarmed totally over the hillside. It took minutes to clear them back, opening the narrowest of lanes down which Junah must hit. Darkness was falling fast as he rifled a mid-iron to the collar of the upper tier. His putt stopped six inches short. He had a bogey, to Jones' and Hagen's pars.

He was one shot back, crossing to eighteen.

By now the darkness had become palpable. At least ten minutes had been lost with the Rules discussion and clearing back the gallery. We crossed the narrow elevated pathway to the tee, with its brand-new carven marker:

18

Valor

Par 5　541 yards

Glimmers of daylight still lingered to landward but to the east, out over the ocean, it was already pure dark. You literally could not see the green, a third of a mile away along the bluff front. Automobile headlights illuminated the landing area of the fairway; more vehicles were being wheeled into position around the green and in the approach areas in front. The wind had stilled with the sunset, but lightning was flashing out over the ocean. "Gentlemen," Dougal McDermott addressed the competitors, "would any of ye lik' tae request a call of play due tae darkness?"

Hagen just laughed. The gallery roared. They would have strung McDermott up by his thumbs had he tried to enforce this. He laughed too. "Then play away, lads!"

The eighteenth ran flush along the ocean, a sixty-degree dogleg left. It was and is, in my opinion, one of the best two dozen holes in the world. And this hour, with the sun beneath the horizon and thunderclaps booming out over the Atlantic, it loomed beyond awesome to apocalyptic. The drive from the championship tee required a carry of 230 over raw duneland, aiming almost at right angles to the green, to a promontory that flared westward, to the right, leaving plenty of bail-out room away from the green. To the left, where a bold shot must travel, was one of the most terrifying but tempting targets a player could imagine. A ball that carried 250 and didn't drift left could cut the steep angle of the dogleg and, if fortune allowed it to thread the narrow lane between the seawall and a row of four pot bunkers, bound forward into perfect approach position, a spoon shot from the green off a clean level lie.

Hagen had the honor. One thing the master never did was allow tension to build, at least not his own tension. Now he stepped to the ball briskly, too briskly, planting and waggling so boldly that he seemed utterly to disdain the hole; the club swept back in a rush, he flailed one that started too far left, flirting with the ocean, then drew even more left. The gallery held its breath as the ball, which was hit hard and long, approached the cut of the dogleg. Would it carry? No! The ball steamrollered down, turning over hard now, landed smack on the seawall and bounded wildly out over the ocean, dead along a line of abandoned concrete pilings, caissons sunk for some long-forgotten jetty. It was too dark to see the splash; we could just glimpse my brother Garland and Tawdry Jones (the forecaddies had doubled up on this final hole) sprinting like madmen toward the point of impact. It made no difference. The Haig was dead.

To his tremendous credit under the circumstances, Hagen remained absolutely jaunty. He plucked his tee from the fast-darkening turf. "This is when a man needs pals in the Mermaids' Union." He winked at two young girls in the gallery, then stepped back. Now Jones came forward.

Every golfer knows the myriad thoughts that can crowd a player's mind at moments like this. With Hagen out of it, a miscue by Bobby could virtually hand the match to Junah. This would be horrific, unthinkable after all that the three of them had been through. I glanced up at my man as I placed Schenectady Slim in his palm. He was in the Field, focused internally, yet I sensed him keenly aware of Jones and rooting for him. He wanted the best possible drive from Bobby. Crush it. Steam it. Tear the cover off it.

Jones swung and nailed it, flush between the screws with all his adrenaline flowing. It was so dark now you could follow the flight only for the first hundred feet, then the white streaking blur melted into black. But the gallery knew Jones had gone all out for the boldest possible stroke and had cracked it perfectly, dead on line for the corner and drawing slightly back to trim the dogleg even tighter. All eyes squinted to the landing slot, illuminated faintly by the auto headlights. You couldn't see; there just wasn't enough light at this distance. Then we heard the cheers; we could make out the spectators beside the cars, heads turning to follow the ball, which was bounding powerfully around the corner of the dogleg. That drive—Garland and I paced it off the next day—measured 320 yards, threading a slot between the bunkers and the seawall that at its widest was no more than eight yards. In the dark.

Junah hammered his drive as hard as Jones but, with the image of Hagen's hook no doubt vividly before his mind, he protected at impact a shade too much against a draw. The ball started to the right, then push-drifted further . . . right, right, so far right that it finished through the fairway, on the upslope of a grass bunker, at least 270 from the now utterly invisible green. The shot was so far off line that I hadn't even paced the yardage last night with Vance. Hiking up to the ball, the only positive thing I could see was that it was so far back there would be no question about which club to pick. It was everything. The whole bag. That or lay up, which was out of the question trailing by a shot. We got to the ball. The lie was good. Enough grass to get the persimmon on it. I squinted toward the green. It was all eye-balling, trying to judge distance in darkness falling so fast you could barely see the flag, even with a dozen autos focusing their headlights upon it. I was just assessing the possible run-up lanes, straight-in all-carry or from the right trying to hook in between the two flanking bunkers, when a cheer and a shout rose from the far left, the seawall. Tawdry Jones was standing atop a concrete caisson, fifty yards out into the surf, waving his white flag theatrically.

He had found Hagen's ball!

There it sat, twenty feet above the pounding breakers, atop the third concrete piling!

The maddest of rushes ensued. Galleryites, officials and marshals swarmed toward the surf's edge. Yes, the ball was playable . . . yes, it was technically still in bounds. There was Hagen, in his $500 shoes, tiptoeing across the rocks with the breakers pounding all around him. His caddie Spec Hammond waded behind, along with two marshals and Dougal McDermott. The spectators whistled and cheered as Hagen took a hand-up from Tawdry the forecaddie and hauled himself up atop the piling.

The caisson summit was concrete, enameled white with gull droppings, and about eight feet square. It was too dark for us to make out Hagen's ball, but from the way he took a stance, practice-swinging without a club, he clearly could get wood on it; it was playable. There was a great deal of shouting up and down between Sir Walter and the officials below, then between him and Spec, who was standing in the surf now with the Haig's gorgeous leather bag descending rapidly to ruination from the salt spray. Junah had given up on remaining detached inside his own game; he and Jones had crossed to a mound where they watched, with O. B. Keeler, like any other spectators. "Later, when he tells the story"—Jones indicated Hagen on his pinnacle—"he'll swear he aimed for the piling deliberately."

"Who knows?" Junah grinned. "Maybe he did."

In point of fact, Hagen's fluke could hardly have been luckier. Out there on the caisson, he had cut the dogleg even more smartly than Jones, taking the surveyor's line to the green and shaving a good fifty yards off the hole. He couldn't have had more than a four-wood left.

Hagen had selected a club now. Yes, it was a wood. Spec was passing it up to him. Along with what . . . ah, Hagen's silver cigarette case. Now the Haig was calling down to Spec, pointing toward the green. What was he saying?

He wanted Spec to attend the pin.

Jones was chuckling deliciously now. Keeler slapped his thighs. The gallery loved it. It took three men to haul Spec up out of the surf; one of the headlight cars gave him a lift to the green on its running board. The sun was now all the way down. It was night. You could see Hagen's cigarette glow as he drew on it, perched atop the caisson fifty yards out into the Atlantic getting ready to address his four-wood to a green surrounded by five thousand fans and illuminated by the headlights of a dozen automobiles.

Spec held the pin. The Haig flung his cigarette into the sea. He addressed the ball, waggled once, then swung. You couldn't hear the ball being struck, not with the surf and the rising wind, nor could you see it, streaking greenward against the black sky. The one thing visible was the Haig in his white shirt and light-gray plus fours, finishing in perfect balance, his best swing of the day.

Then came the cheers. The press reports the following day said the ball carried dead straight, right over the top of the flag, hit ten feet past, took one hop onto the collar and spun back, coming to rest no more than twelve feet above the hole. From where we were, we thought he had holed it. The only way we knew he hadn't was that Spec hadn't pulled the pin. The fans whooped and cheered. You could see the headlights rocking, from the hurrahing galleryites perched on their roofs and running boards.

Now Junah stepped to his ball. The Haig's shot was an impossible act to follow; I could sense Junah rallying from the distraction, recentering within his own game, focusing on the job he had to do. He had the driver. Two-seventy into a chill, solid breeze. There was no choice but to let out every inch of shaft and wail it. He glanced to me as he set his fingers upon the leather. "Hold nothing back," I heard my voice say. "Knock the shit out of it."

Junah grinned. I could see the tension vanish inside him. He set up rock-solid and swung from his heels. The ball boomed off the clubface and vanished into the black. Junah gave me a look. "I can't hit it any better than that," he said.

My father and Garland were by the green then. They told us later that Junah's shot had come in toweringly high, so high it seemed to drop unseen from the ether, tore a huge chunk from the green and tumbled dead, curling in to finish less than a flag length from the hole. Now the headlights really rocked. The galleryites lost all discipline; those who had been with Junah and those who had watched Hagen now surged uncontrollably forward toward the green. Jones stood alone with Keeler amid the stampeding masses; only the two autos that had been brought up to illuminate his ball protected him from the melee. Georgia State Patrolmen and Krewe Island marshals battled the mad rush back. Bobby and Keeler vanished from view, surrounded by the multitude. There were cops around Junah and me too, holding back the fans who were clutching at Junah's sleeves and shouting encouragement.

We couldn't see Bobby swing, couldn't see the shot. All we heard was a third roar from greenside, more tumultuous than the preceding two. Bobby's one-iron, amid all that pandemonium, had struck the apron, taken one bound onto the green, curled left and missed going into the hole by less than six inches. It finished twelve feet past. I feel absolutely secure in declaring that, of all the thousands of rounds played subsequently over Krewe Island's eighteenth hole, no three players ever stood better after two shots apiece.

Now came the putts. Hagen lined up first, asking that the auto headlights facing him be extinguished so he could read the break. This took a good three minutes, as the vehicle owners were either imprisoned inside their cars and couldn't open the doors, the gallery was pressed so tightly upon them, or, in the case of one cavalier fellow, the owner of an illuminated Auburn, insisted before complying on Hagen's signing an autograph. Finally it was done. The Haig had his line. He struck with boldness. The ball rolled fast and straight, rammed itself dead into the back of the cup, then leapt up, bobbled . . . and hung stationary on the rear lip! A cry rose from the gallery that could be heard for a quarter mile. The ball wouldn't fall. Hagen sauntered with infinite slowness, milking every second, hoping for a puff of wind, an earth tremor, anything to jiggle the ball loose that last eighth of an inch. He pantomimed blowing it in, feigned punching it billiard-cue style, even knelt for an extra ten seconds to line up his tap-in. No use. The ball refused to budge. The Haig popped it in, backhand, for his birdie.

Now it was Jones' try for eagle. No histrionics. Just a perfect, achingly tender roll that started four inches above the cup, took the tremulous slippery break down down down, ghosting in on the upper edge of the hole, creeping so slowly that it had to topple in, had it caught even the faintest fringe of periphery. But it didn't. It slipped past, close but not close enough, and curled to a stop like Hagen's, dead behind the hole. Another groan rose from the throats of the five thousand. Jones grinned and tapped it in.

All eyes now swung to Junah. Hagen and Jones had tied, one stroke ahead. This putt, this eagle, would make it a three-way deadlock. With no chance of extra holes or a playoff tomorrow, since both Jones and Hagen had commitments elsewhere, that would be it. Junah would have played the planet's greatest champions dead even.

He asked that all headlights be put out. He would putt by the horizon's afterglow and the lights up the hill from the hotel. Later in the press tent Junah was asked how he read his five-footer in such blackness. "With my spikes," he answered. He meant the soles of his feet. He didn't mention the Field. Or the line that presented itself to his eyes as vividly as if it had been inscribed across the green in incandescent paint.

He just stepped up and rolled it in.

A downhill left-to-right slider, struck not too hard and not too soft, taking the three-inch break and entering the cup smack in the center, front door all the way, to tumble and rattle gloriously in the bottom of the cup.

Pandemonium. In seconds, Jones, Hagen and Junah were swallowed in the mob of frenzied, delirious fans. All three were hoisted onto the shoulders of the throng. It was tumult, raw bedlam. You couldn't breathe, speak or think. Your ears thundered with the cheering and the pounding of your own heart. I remember trying amid the madness to calculate the scores. It was impossible. The brain was functioning entirely from its stem and no higher. It wasn't until an hour later, when the scorecards had long been toted up and signed and I had secured a haven with Garland and my father in the corner of the men's grill, that my brain could return enough to itself to actually think, to tally.

To go with his morning 76, this is how Junah scored:

He had played the final eighteen in 66 strokes, including two balls in the ocean and one self-imposed penalty.

The final nine he had covered in 31.

He had played the last six, as testing a run of closing holes as existed anywhere in the world, in six under par, including the penalty shot on seventeen.

For those six, Junah had gone eagle, birdie, birdie, birdie, bogey, eagle. Against a card of 4 3 5 4 4 5, his scores read

2 2 4 3 5 3

Jones and Hagen had played the last six holes in one under par and lost five shots to Junah.

In the main ballroom of the grand hotel, the press was mobbing the competitors with praise and questions. I looked everywhere for Bagger Vance, but he was gone. I never saw him again.

Twenty-four

I FINISHED THE TALE. The clock on Irene's mantel read 4:17. It was pitch-black outside, with the storm still banging and clattering under the eaves; the children had all fallen asleep on their couches and the fire had burned almost completely down. Michael's eyes in the emberlight were dark with reflectiveness. "Thank you," he said to me, very low. "For what?" I asked, not sure of his meaning. He reached across and took my hand. "You know exactly for what."

Irene too remained preoccupied. Earlier, during a pause in the telling of the story, she had slipped away and returned with several dusty cartons—Junah's scrapbooks and diaries, some of his old handwritten journals and research notes. These boxes now spread before her on the carpet; her fingers absently traced among their forgotten papers.

In the quiet I glanced across at Michael, touched again by the bond I had felt with him since his childhood. Two generations ago, in the South of Junah's day, Michael would have been condemned to a life of servitude. Society would have offered him no alternative. Now here he was, barely a moment later: a stunning athlete in brilliant health, handsome as a god, a doctor or very nearly. The intelligence in his eyes bore none of the reticence of former generations. He held nothing back through deference or diffidence. Yet still tortured . . . by what? Not, I felt, the obvious demons of race or rage. But by the same emptiness, the same barrenness of meaning which had tormented Junah so keenly such a brief few decades ago.

"You mentioned earlier that there was a subsequent event involving Bagger Vance," Michael broke in on these troublous ruminations, "but before we get to that, tell me please, what happened to Junah?" He turned to Irene. "You said he was involved in research concerning navigation, but I'm more curious about him personally. Did he change? And if he was not the same man, how was he different?"

Irene hesitated. You could see that much of the tale still hadn't settled with her either.

"Did he go on playing golf?" Michael asked. "And what happened to Krewe Island? Is any of it still left? Is it playable?"

"Did I hear the word *play*?" Irene swung toward him with a teasing glint. "Don't tell me you're back with us in the game?"

"I didn't say that," Michael replied with a glance toward me. "Though I confess, our venerable physician had me going there for a while, coming down the last few holes." He rose with a great creak and took orders for refills of coffee. "He pretends to modesty but he knows his powers as a spellbinder."

I watched Michael cross behind the counter. His hair was close-cropped in the current fashion and his shoulders showed broad beneath his night-rumpled shirt. "I wish that were true," I said, "but I fear my tale has sputtered out short of the cup, so to speak."

"Finish up about Junah then. What happened to him? I ask you too, Irene, for whatever you can add from memory or notes or your mother's stories."

"There's one thing," Irene answered. "One item that might be of interest to both of you."

She ducked swiftly into the front hallway and tugged open a closet door. It was one of those Fibber McGee closets where kids pack in skateboards and baseball bats, the kind of space where you open the door and volleyballs come tumbling down onto your head. Irene reached deep into the recesses and came out with something. "Have you ever seen this before, Dr. Greaves?"

In the light she held out Schenectady Slim.

"My God. Is that what I think it is?"

She crossed back into the living room and placed the driver in my hands. "My mother had it rebuilt completely a couple of years ago, right down to a new insert handmade from the identical type of hard rubber as the original. It had to be custom-done at Tarry Adair's shop in St. Augustine, the only place in the country that still does this kind of work."

There it was. I could barely believe it still existed. I turned the face over in my hands, astonished at the depth of emotion produced by this simple hickory-shafted weapon. The refinish work was faultless. The craftsman had brought the grain back out, it shone lustrously beneath a dozen coats of clear lacquer; the original soleplate had been rescripted and fitted, even the silk windings around the shaft were threaded impeccably in a duplicate of the original style. I took the grip in my hands and gave the club an easy waggle. There was that same deep face I recalled so vividly, looking as new now with its gleaming clean-grooved insert as it had when I first snatched it from Junah's hotel room the night Bagger Vance and I walked the course at Krewe Island. I was struck by its lively, almost contemporary flexion. "Funny, it doesn't feel old-fashioned at all."

Irene answered eagerly that she had been struck by the same sensation. "Doesn't look old either, does it? It's like that pure classic face has come back around into style."

I became aware of Michael's eyes on the club. I gave him a look. "I'm not sure a nonplayer should be allowed to touch such a legendary instrument." He snorted; I held the grip out to him.

Irene and I stood back as Michael, a little hesitant at first, then gaining confidence as the leather settled within his fingers, took the big long-shafted club and let it find its nestle in his hands. I was struck again by the poetry of Michael's luscious fluid grip, his fine strong fingers recovering the memory they had never really lost. As he flattened his soles into the carpet and settled into an address position between the couch and the fireplace, the flesh rippled electrically up my spine. It was like seeing Junah again, a brother or a comrade-in-arms. I glanced to Irene and felt certain she was sensing some of it too. "I see this one's a player"—she nodded toward me with a grin—"look at the way he sets his meathooks on that shaft."

Michael laughed and gave the stick another sweet, sensitive flex. "Have you ever hit with this club?" he asked Irene.

"I've swung it but never actually hit a ball," she answered. "Listen to this, though: at Adair's shop when they were refitting the shaft, they put it on the frequency meter. Know what material it matched up with almost identically? D-composite graphite!" She laughed with gusto. "It had excessive torque, twenty percent more than the graphite. But that was its only flaw. For kick point, flexion and coefficient of frequency, it was identical to the most technologically advanced shaft in the world."

That seemed oddly appropriate somehow. Michael was turning the clubhead over in his hands now, admiring the purity of its face in the firelight. His fingers ran lightly down the beveled, beeswax-coated shaft. "Something about a wooden shaft, isn't there? I don't know what. Maybe that it was once living. And still is, in a way." He regripped the club and let the hickory talk to him. Maybe he was imagining, as I was, Bagger Vance alone among some chilly stand of Northern hardwood, seeking and finding this one flawless shaft, still with its bark on, still in its raw state of nature. It wasn't hard to picture Vance at work in some lamplit shop, shaping and shaving and tapering, rewarping this slender limb to dead-straight perfection. "Maybe something to do with what Bagger Vance said about intelligence and the hands," Michael said. He pulled up, suddenly awkward and self-conscious. "There's no going back technologically," he said, yielding up the driver at last and passing it again to Irene, "but it's fun to think about sometimes."

The children began to stir on their couches, perhaps from the talk and movement in the room or perhaps from the first creasings of dawn showing outside beyond the high windows. We paused in our conversation and gathered up the little ones in our arms, carried them upstairs and settled them into their own beds. I was struck with Michael's sweetness and moved again by some quality of kinship in his nature, which I had felt so many times since he was a boy.

Downstairs again we took up fresh stations in the kitchen where Michael insisted, with Irene's permission, on whipping up a serious biscuit-and-gravy breakfast. He made us both sit while he brewed fresh coffee. The sky was brightening outside. Irene and I settled on high stools around the counter, warmed by the hot mugs in our hands and the rich smells of eggs and sausage cooking. "If you're not completely talked out"—Michael turned to me—"can you tell us a little more about Junah, about his life after the match?"

It took a moment to return my mind to the past. Then I began.

"I still saw Junah quite often as I grew. He was here in Savannah with his daughter, Irene's mother. He would have supper with my father and mother on occasion; he played in tournaments for charity; I caddied for him a number of times. He liked to play early and late, just himself and Irene's mother, avoiding the crowds and teaching her the game in his own way. Mostly he was just a dad. What I suppose we would call today a single father."

"Did he remarry?"

"Never. Though I don't recall him ever lacking for female companionship, that part of his life, the pursuit of romance, seemed to have lost its luster for him. I can tell you that he went from a man in torment and without purpose to one supremely focused, very nearly to the point of obsession."

Here Irene put in, "Dr. Greaves is right. I remember not so much stories from my mother as just the essence of my grandfather's personality. As I told you before," she addressed both Michael and me, "he was consumed with the coming war and America's need to enter early and with high purpose. He wrote numerous articles, letters to the editor, that sort of thing. I have some in those boxes, they're quite compelling. The voice crying in the wilderness." She paused, recalling something. "There *is* one piece somewhere. Among his notes." She stood and took a step toward the living room. "It may be to the point, Dr. Greaves, because it alludes to that ancient battle. Would you like me to look for it?"

I replied that nothing in the world could interest me more. Please, I begged her, find it. She crossed swiftly to the living room and returned with the boxes; while she began digging, Michael turned to me.

"How did Junah die?"

I started to answer, but the words caught in my throat. "Bagger Vance told him his death would follow quickly," Michael spoke over my hesitation, "which I'm sure must have added urgency to his preoccupations."

"It was in the Second World War," I answered.

Irene followed quickly: "Before America got in."

She continued to Michael as she searched among Junah's papers. "He joined in September of '39, right after the fall of Poland. He could see America's head was still in the sand, so he took a train to Toronto and enlisted in the Royal Canadian Air Force. He was overage but they embraced him in a flash because of his navigation expertise. He insisted on a combat berth. It took a lot of wrangling, I understand, but England was taking a terrible pounding then from the air, and the Allies were desperate for pilots. He was commissioned a major in the RCAF and assigned to an expeditionary unit but only, according to his orders, in a staff capacity. Apparently it didn't take long for casualties to obviate that. He took off from Bristol the day he was killed, flying cover for the last of the Lancaster bombers, and was shot up over the Channel. He rode the plane down. Crashed on a golf course of all places. Sainte-Huguette, in Bretagne. My mother played there once in the French Amateur. Not a bad layout, she said. The French had put up a plaque to honor him and one other plane, Royal Indian Air Force, that went down that same day."

Meaning still seemed to elude us. I felt Michael's silent intensity, as if by sheer will he sought to wring significance from the ether.

Suddenly Irene spoke. "Here they are . . . the notes I was looking for!" She tugged up several handwritten pages, skimmed them quickly to be certain they were the ones she recalled. "Shall I read them out loud?"

As she set the pages before her on the countertop I saw again, for the first time in sixty years, Junah's strong passionate handwriting.

What no one seems to comprehend is that there is only one battle, and that we are compelled by our nature and the nature of reality to fight it again and again. The war that is coming is but the outer reflection of an irresistible inner reality, a reality shared by the mass unconscious of our time. I will fight in this war and the next and the next, as I have fought in the last, and the one before that, and the one before that. I am impelled to this horror, as we all are and will be, until we transform ourselves at last into the incarnation which lies beyond that of the Warrior.

Until we enter the Field, not fleetingly and fallibly as we do now, but at will and with full consciousness. Until those acts which to our limited present vision appear as miracles and wonders are called by their right name, which is nothing more than simple reality. Until we become Magicians, as Bagger Vance is. As all gods are.

The outer world, as he often said and I never understood, is but a shadow play, a dream dreamt not by us but of us. He is dreaming us. And yet he, they, need us to complete the reality we all share, to advance and elevate it into a fuller and greater reality. Continents will shift, as they did after that battle twenty-one thousand years ago. But these are continents not of the planet, but of the Self.

Why did Bagger Vance, possessed of such irresistible powers, reveal himself to me, a man of no great or especial talents? I cannot answer. Why did he take form as a servant, a caddie? I can't answer that either. His love for golf was clearly transcendent, plumbing level after level of meaning, which I could only follow to my poor limits.

During the match at Krewe Island, under that for me terrible pressure, I was unable to assimilate his wisdom or any wisdom. Nothing he said worked, then or later, except one single truth: the fact of his existence and of his love.

That is all I needed then, and all I will ever need.

Irene finished. The pages were contained with several tied bundles of letters in a faded manila envelope. She replaced them now and passed the parcel across to Michael. I could see he was utterly absorbed. Something of Junah had reached him at last. He set all breakfast preparations aside and pored for long moments over the handwritten notes, reading them once and again, and again after that. "I'm sorry, Dr. Greaves"—he suddenly snapped from his preoccupation—"did you want to see these?" I said I did. Michael shuffled the papers square and was just about to reslide them into the manila envelope. "What's this?" he spoke, feeling something. He reached into the parcel, past the bundles of letters.

Up into the daylight came a golf ball.

A bright dimpled Spalding, wrapped in tissue and now popping forth still brilliant white and looking brand new. "It's a Dot," Michael said, squinting at its cover.

I felt my eyes blink. "Is there a *J* on it? A little pen-written *J* just below the numeral?"

Irene was squinting now too. "Damned if there isn't."

They both turned to me.

"It's Junah's ball," I said. "The one he holed out on thirteen. The one Vance holed before him, when he hit those three into the cup."

Twenty-five

WE WERE ON OUR WAY to Krewe Island.

Irene drove in her four-wheel-drive pickup, which seemed the wisest vehicle in the rain and muck. The children had been left in the charge of the two eldest nieces. Rain sheeted before us; Irene's wipers beat and the defroster churned out steamy air. I sandwiched myself in midseat with Schenectady Slim tucked between my knees and Michael's linebacker shoulders propping me on the right. The dawn was showing pearl-gray over the Atlantic. Shredded clouds hid the seaward sun; the road was littered with tree limbs, swamp grass and other assorted storm wrack. "What about Bagger Vance?" Michael addressed me as we took a turn along the waterway, retracing the route we had covered last night. "You said there was one other incident when you thought you saw him."

I responded that I was reluctant. To tell it all now would lead into other areas, areas which for me, for their own reasons, were still extremely painful.

"Oh hell!" Irene cut me off. "Come on, Doctor, you can't take us this far and then back off."

We were searching for the south causeway that once led to Krewe Island. The marshes around us were wild and overgrown, savanna grass higher than the pickup roof and still whipping in the aftergusts from last night's storm. We proceeded down this tunnel of green. I was losing my sense of orientation. There should be an access road here. Wasn't the approach to the causeway right around this curve? The sensation was of eerie and disquieting dislocation: to be certain you recall something, recall it with absolute clarity, not to mention deep significance for your life, then to arrive there, at the precise spot, and find it not at all as you remembered. "The Corps of Engineers has done so much dredging and rechanneling through here"—Irene squinted through the streaking windshield—"I don't know where the hell anything is anymore. Let's stop and climb up on the pickup bed, maybe we can see something over the grass." She pulled onto the shoulder; she and Michael swung their doors open. Just as they were stepping out, a figure passed like a ghost behind me, just out of eyeline.

A man was out there, on Irene's side.

I couldn't see around her but I heard Michael mutter, "Damn." It was the derelict he and I had almost hit last night! Apparently the fellow made his home somewhere in this wilderness. Michael was hissing to Irene to get back into the truck. But she was already in friendly discourse with the wild fellow who, I could just glimpse around her, was pointing ahead and issuing directions with some authority. "He says the road's up here another half mile," Irene called over the wind and storm spray. Michael groaned as the ragged fellow hauled himself up onto the pickup bed behind us. "He says he's going that way himself," Irene said, sliding back under the wheel. "He'll guide us."

"Great," Michael grunted sarcastically, resuming his seat. Our tires hummed out again onto the two-lane.

Irene recalled aloud some of the patchwork past of Krewe Island. Adele Invergordon had held the land for years; at her death it was donated to the State on provision that it be established as a wildlife preserve. Later the Corps of Engineers had attempted to add a link to the Intracoastal Highway but that was blown to hell in Hurricane Camille, 1969. We could hear the ragged fellow rapping behind us now on the pickup roof. He was pointing ahead. There! There was the causeway. As Irene's pickup mounted the frond-littered approach, we could see above the wetlands for the first time. Sure enough, there was the six-mile vista that had been so packed with the motorcade the day Garland and I rode Albert's watermelon truck in the wake of Jones and Hagen. Now all had reverted to nature. The causeway itself was half down in places. As we started toward the distant swell where once Krewe Island's hotel towers had gleamed in the sun, Irene insisted and I began my brief final story.

Twenty-six

"WHEN JUNAH WAS KILLED I was nineteen, in my second year of pre-med at Vanderbilt. The war accelerated everything exponentially. By '43 I was a lieutenant, a Navy M.D. in the Solomons performing ten and fifteen surgeries a day. The closer we got to the home islands, the more ferocious the resistance became. I was on the hospital ship *Bountiful* off Okinawa when the Fifth Fleet took the war's worst casualties under the day-and-night waves of kamikazes. But it was all just prologue to August 6, 1945. Hiroshima."

The road was getting wilder now. Dense grass closed around us; Irene shifted to four-wheel drive and we punched forward, following our guide's instructions into another murky, obscuring tunnel.

"I was assigned to an Emergency Medical Team, sent in even before the official surrender. It was all burn cases. They came in three classes: rare, medium and well done. That was the kind of humor the situation dictated. My point for this story is that I, who had hated the Japanese with a pure and unquestioning passion, now felt the pendulum swing back to include my own side as well. I felt a hatred not just of war, but of mankind in general, making no distinction between 'us' and 'them,' and, on a more secret and vividly conscious level, toward God himself. I hated Him. By now we were seeing wire photos of the bodies stacked outside Dachau and Buchenwald. Then, in the midst of a run of horror-packed eighteen-hour days, I received a telegram from my father informing me that Jeannie had given birth prematurely to our first child. It was a stillbirth. A girl, born dead.

"The Navy couldn't release me. I worked on for another seven months, finally receiving my Discharge and arriving home in Atlanta in March of '46. How can any of us know another's grief? I dwelt in a twilight state beside Jeannie with the act of suicide never more than a membrane away. I couldn't work. Couldn't resume my studies or start a practice. I couldn't read, not even the finest modern authors. Only the ancients. The *Iliad* and *Odyssey*, Shakespeare's sonnets and parts of the King James Bible. I read Ruth's speech to Naomi over and over, weeping every time.

"The only physical activity I could bear was golf. I started just putting. I would pedal out to East Lake alone—the Atlanta Athletic Club had generously given provisional memberships to all returning officers—and putt in the dark, sometimes from two in the morning till dawn. I would slink off in the fog when the first foursomes arrived. Gradually I began to go out, alone or taking just a caddie, very early or very late like Junah used to. I was playing, as Bagger Vance always said, without fear and without hope. Not surprisingly I began to play pretty well. I had never been below a legitimate two, going around in 74 or 75. Now I was rarely over 70 from the extreme backs. Jeannie entered me in tournaments, which I refused to show up for. Finally the Georgia Amateur came to East Lake. There was no escaping. 'They're closing the course for ten days for the tournament,' Jeannie said, 'so if you want to play at all, you have to compete.'

"In my state of somnambulance I breezed through the quarters playing well over my head, squeaked out a one-up nail-biter in the semis, and came up in the thirty-six-hole final against Temple Magnuson, the defending champ. Magnuson was a lawyer from Marietta, a former colonel in the Supply Corps and arrogant as hell. He had me four down at the turn and added two more by lunch. I remember the scorer tugging me aside on the nineteenth tee to ask if I would be kind enough to play the bye holes out. In other words, keep playing for the gallery's sake even after Magnuson had whipped me.

"Up to that point I don't think winning had even entered my mind. I didn't care. Now suddenly I did. The thought that this Supply Corps sonofabitch, this slick barbered bastard who had skated out of the war the same man he was when he entered, who had not endured one millionth of what real soldiers and sailors had, had not even witnessed one millionth of it, that he would beat me, and *forget me*, which seemed even worse, was more than I could bear. I felt in some fevered and no doubt quite deranged way that I was standing in for all those who had suffered, who had been maimed or perished, and that my game must speak for them. This was preposterous of course, but there it was. I felt as if I must win or die, and I no longer wanted to die.

"Whereupon my game utterly deserted me. Like Junah's early collapse. I choked. I clutched. I lost all sense of plane or rhythm. Only by the maddest of scrambling did I stay even through the third nine, and in fact pick up a hole on the thirtieth. I came to the thirty-first five down with six to play. I had the honor and promptly bombed one into the deep timber. The ball was wedged under a root, unplayable. Magnuson strode in midfairway, already accepting congratulations. I had reached my end. I know it sounds silly but this, in some unspeakable way, was the annihilation of my life. I felt my vision swim before me, my eyes began tearing as the waters of despair rose to overwhelm me. I had not thought for months, maybe years, of the match at Krewe Island. Now, as clearly as if he were speaking the words into my ear, I heard Bagger Vance's voice: 'A day will come when you will be drowning. In that hour remember me. I will preserve you.' I knew without a shred of doubt that this was that moment. And I knew exactly what to do.

"I still had my ball, my Spalding Dot, this very ball here in my hand now. It was at home in my dresser. I turned to my caddie, a redheaded urchin named Terry Tucker, whose little brother Mike was tagging behind us. I sent Mike streaking off in his PF Flyers. I had to stall, composing myself and going over my options. Then Mike came huffing back with that Dot. I showed it to the scorer, let him know I would be taking the unplayable-lie penalty, that this was the ball I would be dropping.

"By now of course the whole stunt seemed utterly preposterous to me. What did I expect, some magic from this fifteen-year-old golf ball? The cover would probably peel off the damn thing the second I hit it. I stepped to the shot. Two-ten to the flag, a knockdown hook off half an inch of pine straw that would have to be drilled between two trees no more than four feet apart and somehow stop on a shallow green with deep-lipped bunkers front and rear. How should I hit it? I hadn't the faintest idea even as I settled the two-iron in my grip and sunk my spikes into the crusty, needle-strewn dirt. Something made me look up. There stood Mike, my caddie's kid brother, still gasping for breath after his valiant run. 'Hold nothing back,' his voice said out of nowhere. 'Knock the shit out of it.' "

At this precise point in the story, the road before us ran out. We were well off the causeway now, having four-wheeled past several abandoned gates, followed a number of ancient Corps of Engineers signs, but primarily groping by instinct and the directions of our tattered navigator in back toward the brightening sky over the ocean. Our original dirt two-lane had devolved into a pair of muddy rut tracks. Now suddenly these ended too. "Where the hell are we now?" Irene squinted right and left amid the high, rain-soaked grass.

"Turn left," our guide called from the pickup bed. We looked. There was no road there. No track. No nothing.

"This is crazy," Michael said, his big shoulders broadening with anger. "I'm going to get out and talk to this sonofabitch." His fist was on the door handle.

"Please turn left through here," the derelict man repeated firmly from behind. "I know the way."

The ring of conviction in the man's voice and the surprising forcefulness with which he expressed it silenced all protest, at least for the moment. Irene shrugged and cranked the wheel; we yawed left into raw grassland. "Well, don't stop now." Michael turned to me, no doubt deflecting some of his anger toward our guide in back. "You holed the shot, right?"

I nodded. "I birdied the two after that, winning them both. That was too much for Magnuson. He handed me the thirty-sixth with a bogey and the match was mine, one-up on the thirty-eighth."

I could see Michael frowning. "That was the least of it of course," I said before he could speak. "What changed everything for me, what brought me out of my personal crisis, and what has stayed with me without a moment's failure ever since, was my utter conviction that it was Vance speaking through young Mike. As he had spoken through me on the eighteenth at Krewe Island."

"In other words, you felt . . ."

"I felt what he always made me feel: a sense almost of shame, of awe and mystery and humility. The sense that life was operating by laws of such depth and profundity, and on so many levels that we mortals were ignorant of, that I or Junah or anyone was the meanest form of arrogant fool to yield to the conclusions of despair we invariably allowed ourselves. 'Stand up! Stand up and act!' Vance's voice always insisted."

Michael was eying me dubiously. "And what did young Mike in his PF Flyers have to say about this?"

"I asked him of course, as soon as the match was over, because I knew a boy of his age particularly in those more proper times would never use profanity in front of his elders. I tugged him aside gently, where no one else could hear. 'Mike, I have something very important to ask you. Why did you say "Knock the shit out of it" back there?' The poor little fellow apologized profusely, pleading with me that it was an accident, he had never spoke nothing so frightful in all his life. 'The words just jumped outa my mouth, Doctor, I swear it!' "

Suddenly the track ahead of us opened. What had been blind overgrown jungle widened out onto a dry dune road. There before us shone the Atlantic, crackling gray and wind-lashed as the last battalions of the storm clashed in battle before the pale sun. "There, see? Along the ocean?" Our ragged navigator pointed. "That's the old eighteenth hole."

Michael and Irene squinted through the wipers. Sure enough, you could make out the long dogleg, the seawall and even the shreds of the bunkers where Spec Hammond had waded into the surf to pass a four-wood to Walter Hagen atop his caisson. Michael stepped out of the pickup and turned back to the derelict, who now stood with impeccable posture and composure peering out over the ancient linksland. "How do you know all this?" Michael demanded of the man. "How can you be so damn sure?"

"Because I own this land," the fellow answered with utter understated self-assurance. "Everything you see from here belongs to me."

Twenty-seven

"**Y**EAH SURE, PAL.** " Michael paced angrily along the truck rail. "Sure you own all this."

The stranger was climbing down from the pickup bed. Irene was already out beside the driver's door; I was stepping down on the passenger side. Michael had turned away. "Let's get out of here," he said. "This was a crazy idea, we only did it cause we're all so punchy from lack of sleep." He stepped toward Irene, holding his hand out for the keys.

"You came to play this final hole, Michael," the stranger continued in his cool but emphatic tone. "Don't you think you should do so?"

I still had not seen the man's face. The collar was up on his ragged poncho; the storm hood had obscured my view, nor had I really even tried to look at him, behind us in the pickup bed. Now he stepped down. The rain fell, misting my glasses. I blinked and strained through the beading droplets. . . .

"This is nuts." Michael had turned to Irene, who was gazing curiously, held by something in the strange man's presence. "Who is this guy? How does he know why we came here . . . and how does he know my name?"

"I have known you under many names, Michael."

I tore my glasses off. The man turned. I saw his face.

"Are you all right, sir?" He reached to take my elbow. Apparently I had staggered. I blinked and stared into the stranger's bottomless eyes. . . .

It was Vance of course.

As part of me had known as early as last night on the road, and surely had known now for the past twenty minutes.

"Let him alone, you!" Michael shouldered the lean stranger aside, moving in to support me. Michael turned to Irene. "I've had enough of this business. What are we even doing here? We're certainly not marching down there in this muck!"

Michael's angry gesture took in the ragged line of Krewe Island's long-neglected eighteenth. The hole, what remained of it, was literally a pasture. A field. My gaze stayed riveted on Vance. He had not changed one iota nor aged one degree. His eyes glowed just for a moment with a private light for me. Then he turned to Michael. "The hole looks fine to me," he said.

We all turned. Someone's trespassing sheep were just now shambling off to the far right, the bail-out zone of the old fairway. I found myself recalling what Keeler had said, the night he and Vance had stood silently, peering out over the darkened duneland. Krewe Island despite the years had not reverted to nature; her identity was stamped so strongly upon her, the hole seemed if possible more itself than ever. The grazing beasts had maintained the fairway. The bunkers along the seawall had been gouged deeper by years of storm and disuse, but in an odd Scottish way that only made them more authentic. The hole had matured. Where the duneland grass grew wild, it looked like the raw carries a player faces at Prestwick or Carnoustie. The worn storm-settled undulations contributed a smack of Western Gailes; Nairn and Troon were there in the sharp wind and over all like a bright patina was the wild, scudding-cloud light of Royal Dornoch. In a savage sea-torn way the land had at last become Krewe Island, Invergordon's dream.

"It doesn't look half bad." Irene squinted out over the shore. Her hand held Junah's rebuilt persimmon. Michael made a face.

"You're not really going down there?"

"Why not? We came all this way."

"We don't have spikes. We'll be slipping on wet grass; my God, the fairway's half sheep and cow shit!"

"I don't know why," Irene said, "but I want to hit this ball." She held her grandfather's '31 Spalding Dot.

I held mine in my hand too.

"Here, Michael," Vance spoke very softly. "I saved the third for you."

He held out another brilliant 1931 Spalding. Still white, still new. With the pen-marked *J* beneath the numeral.

Michael staggered. Irene fell back too. I thought both their eyes would start from their sockets. "What the hell is this!" Michael turned to me, furious. "Is this some kind of joke, Doctor? Because I don't find it funny at all."

I denied this instantly and profusely. But I felt my own brow flushing with shock and confusion. . . .

"The path looks dry"—Vance took a step forward—"let's go down to the tee."

Lightning flashed over the ocean. My whole back was gooseflesh. I saw Michael's glance seek mine. Vance started forward; Michael caught his arm, hard. "Who are you?" he demanded with a harshness unlike anything I had ever heard in his tone. "I'm not taking a step down this path till you tell me what the hell is going on!"

The warrior god turned to him. He was as tall and lean as Michael was muscular, as poised and centered as Michael was spooked. "You will know me in every age," he said, "by the way deluded men respond to me. They despise me, as you yourself did when we first met on the road."

"That's not true!" Michael shot back, hard and defensive. "I was only upset because . . ."

He pulled up, tripped by guilt and truth. He knew now, and so did Irene. She moved in beside Michael, reinforcing. "Where did you get that ball?" she queried Vance, barely containing the tremor in her voice. "How did you . . . ?"

"The ball is for you, Michael," Vance spoke, eyes never leaving the young athlete's. "You are why I have come. You are why I am here." He placed it gently into Michael's palm.

Vance turned and stepped onto the path that led down to the

eighteenth tee. Michael wheeled in disquiet toward Irene; she clutched his free hand. Irene's glance shot back to me, clearly pleading, *What should we do?*

"I don't know about you two," I said, "but I'm going to play the hole."

I started down the path behind Vance. Now I could smell him. How had I missed it before? That raw keen animal smell that was beyond wildness, to humanity in its deepest, most primordial sense. A sudden fear gripped me; that Michael and Irene would freeze . . . and flee. "Don't look back"—I heard Vance's calm voice—"they will follow."

The tee itself, when we tightroped across the last worn crest of path, was dry and cropped as close as a putting green. The links turf grew dense and tight underfoot; even my loafers found sure, easy purchase. I peered down the fairway. From this new vantage with the surf beneath us and the wild dawn light behind, the hole looked like the greatest of Scottish links do, as if crafted by forces far wiser than man, natural as a riverbed, pure as daybreak. "Does it remind you of anything, Hardy?" Vance asked in his still, gentle voice. I knew of course what he meant.

"Of the thirteenth green," I answered, "that day you stopped the sun."

He turned with a smile and laid his hand upon my shoulder. Instantly the rush of warmth that I remembered so well flooded over my bones. His face, which I like Michael had passed over at first without a glance, now shone magnificent in its warriorlike brilliance and beauty. "You've earned the honor, Hardy. Please," he said, "play first."

Michael and Irene had indeed followed us down; now they stepped tentatively off the path onto the tee. You could see their astonishment at the turf's pristine condition. Even the ancient tee marker remained readable with its worn letters and numerals carved into the wood.

18
Valor
Par 5   541 yards

I teed my ball and stepped back. "Take no practice"—I heard Vance's voice behind me—"simply hit."

I obeyed. It surprised me not at all to flush the ball dead between the screws and watch a hard ripping rocket boom off the clubface, ride the following wind and steam down to land just right of the seawall bunkers, and bound ahead strongly around the neck of the dogleg. Exactly like Jones' drive, only lacking fifty or so yards of his distance.

Vance's eyes summoned Irene next. She teed her ball uncertainly, glancing to Michael and me for reassurance, then gripped her grandfather's long-shafted driver. It was a serious weapon, even for him, and for a moment I feared that she wouldn't be able to handle it. Foolish. She drew the big persimmon back in a strong slot-grooved motion and pounded a beauty, along the same line as mine and every inch as long. She stepped away with a look of wonder, even fear, eyes flicking first to Vance, then back toward Michael, who now stood at the edge of the tee with the rain beading on his handsome face and the wind sheeting across his eyes.

"Forget it," he spoke directly to Vance. "I'm not taking part in this freak show, or whatever crazy stunt you think you're pulling. . . ."

Irene reached for him. "Do it, Michael."

"I won't"—he tugged free—"don't ask me!"

Irene glanced anxiously to me. I had no idea what to say. "It's all right," Vance spoke evenly. "I understand the young man's hesitation. Do I have your permission then," he asked him, "to hit the shot for you?"

"Do whatever you want, it makes no difference to me," Michael answered.

Vance stepped before Irene and held out his hand for the driver. "You're wondering how long this land has belonged to me," he addressed her as she placed the weapon across his fingers. "There was never a time when it did not." He held out his palm to Michael, who with a shudder dropped the third ball into it. Vance bent and teed it. But he was not aiming down the fairway.

He was aiming out to sea.

Now his brilliant hands settled around the leather. A part of me, I confess in candor despite it all, had still held out like Michael in disbelief; this couldn't be real, couldn't truly be happening. Now I saw his hands and all doubt vanished. It was his grip. Vance's perfect, magnificent grip. My glance shot to Michael. "Michael is reluctant," Vance spoke as he stepped to the ball and set the driver that he himself had fashioned behind it, "because he is thinking with his head. He knew better as a boy. He knew that here, in the hands, is where true intelligence resides. The swing exists in all its perfection within the grip already, as our lives exist entire in every present moment."

Vance swung.

It was his swing. I knew it would be, but memory, no matter how vivid or recently rehearsed, could not prepare me for the power that poured from his slender sinewy frame. To the top in perfect balance; the slightest pause and then Schenectady Slim dropped down into the slot; Vance's legs drove through with impeccable economy and then with mind-shuddering might his hands unleashed their full lashing fury. The sound of the ball exploding off the clubface made Irene gasp. Our necks snapped trying to follow its blurred, blasting fight. "My God," Michael's voice uttered numbly behind me. The ball streaked and flew, rising with spectacular power to the point when it must peak and begin its gravity-driven fall. But it didn't fall. It climbed and rose and rose some more, boring into infinity, to the seething heart of the storm. Lightning flashed in four directions as the ball vanished and the clouds roiled and tossed in fury.

Michael stared dumbstruck as Vance rocked back out of his finish and settled again onto his soles before him. "You have heard Hardy speak of that ancient battle," he addressed Michael directly, "and you dismissed it as harmless tale or metaphor. It was no metaphor, Michael." Vance stepped before the young man now and placed a hand on his shoulder. I saw Michael stagger. Irene and I sprung forward to steady him. For a moment I thought Vance would dismiss us. But he seemed somehow to want, and even need, us there. I braced myself on Michael's left; I could feel Irene do the same on the right.

"The battle," Vance spoke now, directly to Michael, "marked a day not of glory, but of tragedy. Civilization stood then, as it does now, in the twilight of an aeons-long cycle. Like us, those vanished warriors planted their standards in the sands of their own self-summoned extinction."

Vance gestured out over the vanished seafront, above the booming ocean.

"The fact of battle, as each man grasped painfully in his heart, was proof of the race's failure. They knew, warriors and dreamers and magicians, that bright as their comet had shown, it had fallen short through its own failure of nerve and self-compassion. Mankind must now quench in blood and horror the unresolved fury of its soul. I strode among the warriors, filling each with the courage to meet his destiny. Do you remember, Michael? Can you see the field of battle before you now?"

Michael's glance was wild, tormented, peering straight into the heart of the storm, to ocean that once had been land, to land that had once been battlefield.

"The first I found was Junah," Vance spoke, "eldest and most keenly conscious, beside his chariot at the forefront of the battle line. He pleaded with me for mercy, for foe as well as friend. I ignored him, spreading before his grasp the weapons of his destiny. His hand seized a bow of burnished ash and arrows of fletched steel, murderous and invincible."

Michael trembled before the warrior god's power. His eyes

showed white beneath flickering lids; Irene and I held him tight, supporting . . .

"Next I sought out Hardy, a generation younger than Junah. I found him too, in infantryman's armor, torn with the grief of his own and his brothers' failure. He begged me in the name of humanity to forbear. Him too I ignored and again displayed my weapons. In pain he grasped a bronze-bound oak battle spear, its killing point merciless and insuperable."

Michael reeled and shuddered, without doubt seeing this all with the inner eye. "Then I found you." Vance stepped now, moving directly before him. "Youngest of the three, last in the line of generations and blessed with the greatest strength and compassion. You too pleaded for the race, and before you too I arrayed the shafts of your destiny. Do you remember?"

Michael stiffened as if blasted by a charge; Irene and I held him firm between us.

"Do you remember what you chose?" Vance repeated, and we could feel Michael shudder yet again.

"I do," the young man said, and his whole body seemed to convulse from the charge and current of this remembered vision. I could feel the voltage, like a wave, rush from his sole to his crown.

"It was neither bow nor spear," Vance spoke with his absolute centered quietude, "but a plain wooden staff, the staff of physic. From time immemorial the shaft of mercy, whose power is not to kill but to heal."

Michael's knees buckled. Vance's words had cut through to

his heart. His eyes sprung open; he began to weep. He buried his face in Irene's shoulder, clinging to her with all his strength.

"You I gifted with the most demanding but exalted destiny of all. Yours was to move among the maimed and wounded, bearing comfort and surcease from pain. Your charge was not to slay but to heal, not to rend but to make whole.

"That was the destiny you chose then," Vance declared, "and the destiny which chooses you now. Stand up."

Thunder boomed over the ocean. Michael struggled to rise; clinging to Irene, with help from me, he found his feet. "Stand now!" Vance's voice thundered with necessity. Michael obeyed, trembling. I was struck as if seeing it for the first time by his youth and strength, his beauty. He was like Junah, only stronger and more graceful. Like me, if I may say so, only kinder and with deeper mercy.

Vance held out Junah's great hickory-shafted driver. "Four is the number of completion. The number of wholeness."

In his hand he held a fourth ball.

Michael took it and teed it.

His hands were trembling as he set them upon the leather of the driver's grip. There was vision and power in Junah's warrior club, and now that charge poured its raw voltage into Michael. Up the living shaft the magic trembled. I saw again the young man's pure and brilliant grip. It was the grip of his boyhood, the flawless sweet structure of tendon and bone, tissue and fascia and flesh. Vance was right. All of Michael's swing, all of this life and all his future lives lay compassed already within that pure perfect grip. Michael's eyes met mine just for an instant, clear and purposeful. He set the clubhead behind the ball and waggled once, the toes inside his shoes gripping firmly into the thick dense turf. The Field settled around him, swallowing him in the vorticed web of authenticity. Michael took one smooth easy inhale, then slowly, effortlessly, impeccably, he started the mighty clubhead back. . . .